KARAOKE NIGHT

John Watson

KARAOKE NIGHT

KARAOKE NIGHT
A supernatural horror

A Killer Tune

Ten songs.
Ten tales.
One creepy town.

John Watson

For Penny.

My love, my muse, my happily ever after.

Foreword by Jeffrey Miller

A Story is Born

As a writer, one of the questions that I am frequently asked is how I come up with the ideas for my novels. Sometimes they might come from something that I've read in the news, a snippet of a conversation I overheard, or maybe the idea will be some memory buried deep in my subconscious that eventually took root and sprouted into a story. No matter what process brings the inspiration, the result is always the same: a story is born.

While I was reading John Watson's brilliant literary styling, *Karaoke Night*, I thought about this several times wondering how he came up with the ideas and the individual stories which make up this novella. I had to admit, just the idea of somehow connecting karaoke with a story was ingenious enough—but to have one story seamlessly segue into the next (yes, like someone singing one song after another at a karaoke!) was masterful, to say the least. But knowing John Watson for as long as I have, it is what I have come to expect with his writing.

I first met John back in 2008 on this online writing community called This Is By Us—better known affectionately as TIBU. Members could upload poems, stories, and essays and then other members would comment and "like" them. More importantly, the more "likes" one got for their submissions, as well as interacting with other members, earned them pennies (yes, real pennies, which were eventually paid to authors when the site folded in 2009). However, what made TIBU such an interesting online place was all the support writers could get, as well as feedback, and in the process, new friendships were forged—many which have lasted to this day.

John was one of my first TIBU friends who went by the online name, "inkedwriter." Already having something in common—our fondness for tattoos and New Wave/Punk Rock music—we soon, by the very nature of TIBU's platform, began to read each other's work. One of his stories that still resonates with me today was one about a tattoo artist who uses his own blood as the "ink" for his tattoo creations. That's when I realized John was a masterful storyteller and capable of great things—which brings you and I full circle to why John asked me to write this foreword to *Karaoke Night*.

First of all, I have to confess, I absolutely LOVED the idea behind this novella. I like the format of the book, in the form of "interviews," and how John used various songs to, in some ways, embody the personalities of the characters being interviewed. And I also like the irony of the idea of karaoke—something that we would associate with having a good time, but in the context of this book, that's not the case. Here the karaoke is where the characters bare their souls and lay to rest the ghosts of their troubled pasts. Not actually what you would call a good time, but they are the book's strength that keeps you engrossed from one page to the next.

From the opening stories, "Strawberry Fields Forever" and "Dancing Queen" (my favorites) to "School's Out" and "King of the Road," these stories will hook you with their evocative and haunting underpinnings. You know how some people say that a certain favorite song of theirs would be the soundtrack for their lives? Well, that's what you get with *Karaoke Night* and the songs that underpin the character's lives. And if you can hear these songs playing in your head as you read, well, that's just one more reason why this book will hook you and keep you riveted until the very end.

Bottom line, *Karaoke Night* is a powerful debut book.

Welcome to the show, John.

Jeffrey Miller,

Ice Cream Headache

Track Listing

Intro by the author

Strawberry Fields Forever by Paul

Dancing Queen by Ursula

Barracuda by Neil

Bad to the Bone by Ian

Coal Miner's Daughter by Susan

One Bourbon, One Scotch, One Beer by Harold

Piece by Piece by Marie

This Flight Tonight by Eric

School's Out by Norm

Love Shack by Tanya

King of the Road by unknown

Outro by the author

Intro

A little over a year ago, I went missing for 72 hours. I remember nothing during my time off the radar, yet I have a digital recorder that holds a series of interviews held during that lost period. These recordings offer some clues as to my whereabouts for those three days, but I quickly discovered that all the roads those clues took me on led to nothing but dead ends.

I am getting ahead of myself here, as it's probably a good idea that I tell you why I was out on the road in the first place. My name is Brian Keane, and while I tell people that I am a writer, the reality is that I am little more than a glorified blogger. Before the release of this book, I had never had any of my work published, although I do possess a rather lovely collection of rejection letters that run the gamut from sweet and kind to bitterly acerbic in tone.

The writing niche that I carved out for myself came in the form of a popular travel blog. There is no point in my telling you more about my little piece of real estate on the internet, as it has long since been taken down, a move that my publisher believed would make me all the more mysterious ahead of the launch of this book. I miss updating that blog on a daily basis, although the hefty advance that I received takes some of the pain away.

While it is certainly thrilling to find myself among the ranks of the published authors, I find myself in a bit of a quandary. The book you are about to read is not, regardless of how the marketing machine at my publishing house sells it, a work of fiction. I may not remember giving the interviews contained within these pages, but I also know that I did not plan them or pay voice actors to help me create a pre-planned script. I only wish I were that clever.

What I do know is that I ended up in a town called Redfield in the heart of rural Georgia. How I landed in that town is a mystery, as my last clear memory is of following a dirt road that was pointed out by a broken down, old wooden sign that read, "Karaoke Night." Since the goal of my trip was to write a piece about lesser known dive bars in Georgia, the sign seemed like one that was heaven sent. The mystery here is that Redfield does not appear on any maps of the state, but that is something that I will get into a little later.

Based on the digital recordings, as well as some handwritten notes in my travel journal, it seems as though the people at the karaoke night were in the habit of singing the same songs, over and over and over again. I understand that people who get up on stage to belt out a tune will more often than not choose one that paints their voice in the best light possible. That said, folks also tend to have a couple of tunes in their repertoire, and they certainly don't sing the same song more than once on a given night. I needed to understand why this was happening, but

I certainly did not expect the stories that were related to me.

The stories told here are all taken directly from the recordings, although some parts were muffled or otherwise unintelligible. I wanted to give as true a representation as possible when relating these stories, but since the publisher seems intent on pushing this as a work of fiction, I went with the advice of my wife and took some liberties in the recounting. I promise, the changes are small and do little to affect the overall theme of each tale.

I have some other things to tell you all, but it is perhaps best to save those details for the end. I will save you some time and tell you not to bother Googling the events outlined in this book. You will only find the same level of disappointment and frustration that I felt when I tried to validate the transcripts you are about to read. It's as though the town of Redfield, and the people who lived there, disappeared as mysteriously as I did last year.

The only thing left for you to do now is read on and formulate your own opinions. Is all of this real, or I am spinning a yarn to you now, reeling you all in with a tale of woe about not being believed by anyone other than my wife? I know the answer, but I will leave it up to you to decide how you feel. Maybe, just maybe, I will be able to sway the pessimistic among you when we talk again at the end of this book.

Strawberry Fields Forever by Paul

BK: Please have a seat and tell me a little about yourself.

Paul: What's that thing?

BK: Oh, it's a digital recorder. I want to record your story and perhaps use it in my blog, assuming you are okay with that.

Paul: I guess I don't mind. It's not as though anyone is going to believe what I tell you anyway. I'm not even so sure I should be sitting here talking to you about anything.

BK: It's entirely up to you. Why don't you start by telling me your name and a little bit about what you do in this town?

Paul: No harm in that, I guess. Name's Paul. I've lived in Redfield since the day I was born, which would be 47 years now. My family started the strawberry plantation that this town was built on. The business has been handed down through the years. I ain't smart enough to run it on my own, so I pay some clever folks to do the money stuff while I do the hard labor. It's honest work, and I enjoy it well enough.

BK: So, that's why you sing Strawberry Fields Forever?

Paul: If that were the case, it wouldn't be much of a story, now would it? I wouldn't have felt the need to sit here and share spit with you if all it was about was my working in a strawberry field since I was knee-high to a grasshopper.

BK: My apologies, Paul. Would you be willing to tell me why you sing that particular song then?

Paul: I guess.

BK: Whenever you are ready, Paul.

Paul: Back when I was a kid, in the days before my old man put me to work, those strawberry fields were my playground. Our home and backyard were small, but they butted right up onto the field. Right smack dab in the center of all those strawberries was a beat up old pick-up truck. The weather had long since taken off the outside paint, with nothin' but rust holding the whole thing together. She wasn't pretty to look at on the outside, but her interior was somethin' else altogether.

BK: Can you describe it to me?

Paul: I don't see why such a thing would be important, but I guess I could. I remember it clear as day how it looked and felt, how the shiny buttons and interior trimmings all seemed at odds with how she looked from the outside. She was, and still is, the ugly girl with a heart of gold.

BK: So, the truck is still there, out in the field?

Paul: Of course. She's a permanent fixture, although I've often thought about having her taken away after all that happened. I'm not saying it's her fault entirely, but the passenger she carries is not something you want to mess with, no sir.

BK: Passenger?

Paul: This story is gonna take some time to tell if you keep on butting in. Not that it matters. I ain't got nowhere else to be, but judgin' by how folks in here are looking at us, I got a feeling you are gonna have some company for a while. Everyone here has a story to tell, and it looks like they are all itchin' to get a turn.

BK: I have as much time as you all need, Paul. Please, take as much time as you need to tell your story in detail, and I'll do my best to avoid interrupting. I confess it's a bad habit on my part.

Paul: Fair enough then. Let me go back to the truck before I talk about her hitchhiker. That vehicle was the first love of my life, long before I noticed the wigglin' and jigglin' of the fairer sex. Let's be honest, you usually gotta wine and dine a lady before she allows you inside. Not this truck. She was as welcomin' as could be right from the get-go. I slipped on in whenever I felt like it, and I could always tell that she was happy to have me on board. The same was true of my best buddy, Calvin. He was my twin brother, but I always thought of him as a pal more than a brother. We were inseparable, and that truck was our doorway to other worlds.

BK: Can you tell me about some of those new worlds?

Paul: Uh-huh. My momma died giving birth to Calvin and me. I was the first one out, and I got outta there without a hitch. Calvin was a bit more trouble, as he was looking to escape feet first. Redfield is just a small town. The doctor here wasn't ready for no complications or diversions from the norm, so he hacked Momma up real bad trying to get Calvin out. It took some time, and she lost a lot of blood, way too much to come back from, I guess. Momma passed away on the delivery room table, and I swear my old man died at the same time. He blamed Calvin for Momma's passing. Pops never said so out loud, at least not when he was sober, but he treated us differently. Calvin would get a whoopin' for things I did; the old man refused to believe that I could have been responsible, not with a known troublemaker and momma murderer livin' under the same roof.

BK: I'm sorry.

Paul: What you got to be sorry for? It's Calvin that deserves the apologies, but he ain't around to hear them no more.

BK: I didn't mean…

Paul: As soon as the sun came up, Calvin and I would head out to the truck. He would yammer on about the adventures we could go on once we got there. He was the smart one of the two of us. My guess is that he somehow swallowed up some of my brains when we were in Momma's belly together. Anyway, depending on the story he came up with on any given day, the truck would become a spaceship exploring the stars or a tank goin' into battle. My favorite was when Calvin would talk about the truck bein' a submarine. The big steering wheel in there seemed just right for that story. I would crank that bad boy and pretend we were avoidin' coral reefs, torpedoes, and all manner of things that could have torn our sub to pieces. We'd spend all day out there, chowin' down on strawberries for lunch. Once that sun started dippin' down, and the sky turned red, we knew it was time to head on home.

BK: Would your father get angry if you were late?

Paul: Heck, no. As long as we weren't comin' home in the back of a police car, he didn't care when we got back. We pretty much had to fend for ourselves when it came to eatin' and such. We were lucky in that some of the women from the other families in town would drop off food that just needed to be heated up. It was the passenger in that truck that made sure we were never out there when it was dark. He was the one to fear, not Pops.

BK: I don't mean to pressure you, but can you tell me about the passenger you keep referring to?

Paul: I guess, but this is the part of the story where I might start to lose you. There ain't a day goes by that I don't think about Calvin and that truck. I see it out in that field every day, hear it callin' to me, but I also see the passenger lookin' my way. He wants me over there, but I know better than to give him the time of day. Our Calvin did, and things didn't turn out so well for him.

Our family depended on the money made during the strawberry season, which meant we needed to make sure that our fields were free from pesky birds and wrigglin', hungry insects that loved the taste of that sweet fruit. Pops paid one of the locals to fly a crop duster over the fields. You could hear that old bird comin' from miles away. Calvin and me weren't supposed to be in the fields when the plane made a pass, but we would sometimes hunker down in the cabin of the truck and pretend that our tank was takin' enemy fire. We never had any problems with the chemical shit he was sprayin', so we thought nothin' of it. The duster solved the insect problem, but it was the passenger who took care of the birds.

BK: I'm still not sure I understand.

Paul: That's because I ain't explained it to you yet. How can you understand when you ain't been told the full story? The passenger lived in the bed of the truck. Pops told us that his old man was responsible for the thing in the back. He said that grandpa would be out there for days on end, taking potshots at crows with his old buckshot rifle. It seems he did more damage than good, oftentimes blastin' great chunks out of the crop when he missed the birds. It seems he got it into his head that a scarecrow would be better than blowin' up strawberries, so he drilled a big hole in the bed of the truck, jammed a sturdy stick in there, and mounted himself a scarecrow. By all accounts, them birds steered well clear once that big bastard made of straw took up residence in the bed of that truck.

BK: Was it really that scary?

Paul: To tell you the truth, he wasn't much to look at, but it was when you weren't lookin' that things got odd. He was just your average scarecrow; a bundle of straw-filled sacks dressed up in a plaid shirt and jaunty hat. He had eyes made of black buttons, with bright white thread used to hold them in place. The weird thing was that the thread always stayed perfectly white. No amount of shitty weather or dust storms could change the shade of that thread. It always made those button eyes seem lifelike, and you would feel as though they were followin' you when you were in his line of sight.

The icin' on the scarecrow cake, though, was the scythe that he held. You could never tell how he was able to hold onto the knotted wooden handle. It was as though it was held on by magnets, but I ain't so dumb that I don't know that magnets don't attract wood. It stayed in his hand, though, and the blade on that thing may have looked rusted and worn down, but it was as sharp as a city slicker's suit. Calvin once threw an apple at that scarecrow, hitting the scythe instead of the head. That apple sliced right in two, and while neither of us said it out loud, we both knew the scarecrow moved that blade to cut old Granny Smith to the core.

BK: Surely it was just your imagination. Scary things seem that much more real when you are little.

Paul: I know I said I ain't smart, but I also ain't in the habit of makin' shit up that ain't real. I don't give a flyin' fuck what you believe or don't believe. You wanted my story, and I'm givin' it to you. Use what you want and toss out the rest, or don't use any of it at all. I don't care, but I'm tellin' you, if you make me stop now, you'll miss the best part, the part that eats away at my gut and brings nightmares, even when I'm wide awake.

BK: I'm sorry. I…

Paul: Quit apologizin' and just shut the fuck up and listen. I want this over with quicker than you do. This story ain't somethin' I've ever spoken out loud, but when I saw you sittin' here, listening to my song ever so closely, I just felt I had to tell you. Perhaps it's you bein' a stranger that makes me want to get this shit off my chest. Perhaps it's the fact that I've been carryin' it around forever, the weight of it draggin' me down, knowin' that everyone in here knows all about it, but never sayin' a word or askin' how I'm doin'. Let me get it out so that you can move on to the next story. Don't think I don't see that rug muncher hoverin' around waiting to get in here next.

BK: Who?

Paul: You'll find out soon enough. I'm about at the end of my time here, so let me jump ahead to the main part of the story. I could sit here and talk about Calvin all day, but nothin' I say or do is gonna bring him back. I see him in my thoughts all the time, but the way I see him the most is on that last day. It's probably guilt that keeps takin' me back to that shitty day. We might both be dead now if I had helped, but bein' dead probably feels a whole lot better than how I feel most nights, especially here, singin' that song. I need to do it, though, I need to, you understand?

The night before Calvin left for good, Pops went on a bit of a bender. One of our neighbors would whip up a batch of moonshine every so often, and he would always drop a bottle off for Pops. You could smell that stuff as soon as he popped the cork. That shit would burn your nostrils from way across the room. I can't imagine what it did to the old fella's guts, but he swallowed it down like it was spring water served up on a summer day. Anyway, he nodded off with the TV on, which meant we got control of what to watch. Not too many options back then, but we landed on a documentary about the war. They were talkin' about a big battle in some place in Europe and how all these poppies grew in the fields where there was so much bloodshed. Calvin got real quiet durin' that show and I could see his brain workin' overtime. I knew we were in for somethin' special that next day out in the truck. You okay there, fella? You look a little green around the gills.

BK: Um, yes, I'm...I'm fine. This story just isn't going how I expected.

Paul: I suspect things might get a little worse for you before all of this is said and done, and I don't just mean with my story. Are you sure you're up for this? I mean, all of this?

BK: Yes. Please continue.

Paul: Well, that next mornin', we woke up to the blackest skies we had ever seen. It was like all the blue had been sucked away, lettin' outer space poke on through just a little bit. Calvin turned on the radio, and we listened to the news fella talking about how our area was under a tornado watch, and about how everyone should stay home until it had passed. I was all for that, but not Calvin. He had a story cooked up, and he couldn't wait to play it out in the truck. He was bein' all secretive that day, or maybe he was trying to make me go, but he said he wouldn't tell anythin' about the story until we were in the cabin of the truck.

BK: Did you and Calvin have a name for the truck?

Paul: What kinda dumbass question is that? I swear, it's like you're intentionally tryin' to stop me from finishing the story, tryin' to extend my pain a little. You some cruel asshole that gets their jollies from other people's pain? Because if that's the case, you are in for some fun here in Redfield.

BK: No, Paul. Honestly, I'm just trying to get the whole picture.

Paul: Okay then. Well, we get out to our nameless truck and Calvin starts to fill me in. We are a pair of tank commanders stormin' the fields in Europe. He told me to imagine that the strawberries were poppies, sayin' it would make the whole thing seem more real. It got real very quickly, as that wind started whippin' up and tossin' the truck this way and that. I ain't gonna lie, I was scared, but I was also gettin' caught up in the story and the way Calvin was actin' like a real war hero. It took a minute to realize that it was a tornado warnin' we were hearin', not an air raid siren. That's how deep we were in.

Anyway, by the time we snapped back to reality, there was a big twister heading our way. The truck was really rockin' by this point, and the windshield was getting' splattered by strawberries that were gettin' sent flyin' in the wind. Calvin had this look on his face that's hard to explain. It's like he thought this was the coolest thing he had ever seen, but I was just shittin' myself. The tornado was movin' fast. I made the mistake of lookin' out the window at the back of the truck. As soon as I turned, I found myself face to face with the head of the scarecrow. The body was still standin' upright, but the head had been torn off. Those black button eyes were more alive than ever, and that was the end for me. I remember yelling at Calvin to come on before I jumped outta that truck and made a beeline back to our house. We had a big storm cellar under the house, and that's where I headed.

BK: What about Calvin?

Paul: Well, when I got home, Pops was comin' chargin' out the door like a man possessed. He was screamin' at me to get inside and down into the cellar. I told him that Calvin was still out there, but he paid me no mind. He locked the front door and said there was nothin' we could do for him now, and that it was in the hands of Mother Nature.

It felt like we were down there forever, but it was probably no more than ten or fifteen minutes. I remember that the sound was deafenin' when the storm was rollin' by, but then it got real quiet. I wanted to get out there and find Calvin right there and then, but Pops made me stay down there a little while longer. When we did finally get out, I went tearin' off towards the truck. It's the strangest thing, but the first thought I had as I got closer was about how that damn scarecrow had been able to get its head back in place. It wasn't until I got real close that I saw the truth. Calvin's head was wedged onto that busted ass body, his eyes all glazed over and his mouth hangin' slack.

BK: Jesus!

Paul: No, I'm pretty sure he wasn't there that day. The good Lord and Savior would not have allowed that to happen to my brother. I collapsed on the ground, sobbin'. I remember Pops pickin' me up and carryin' me home, tellin' me everythin' was gonna be okay, even though I knew it never would be again. He went back out later with a couple of friends lookin' for the rest of Calvin, but they never did find his body. I heard them talkin' that night, all fucked up on moonshine, talkin' about the blood on the scythe and how a freak accident must have happened.

Here's the crazy thing, though; the thing that keeps comin' back to me. As time passed, the details of how that whole thing looked after the storm started comin' back, and I clearly remember the cabin being soaked in blood. I asked Pops about it when I was a little older, and he said it was the juice from the strawberries. It seemed like a fair enough excuse to pass off on a kid, but how did those strawberries get in when all the windows of the truck were still in one piece?

BK: Did you continue to live there after all this happened?

Paul: Of course. Where were we gonna go? Pops had a business to run, and that meant groomin' me to take over some day.

BK: What about the truck and the scarecrow?

Paul: Both are still there. I never did set foot in that truck again, although I did look inside one time. It was as bright and shiny on the inside as I always remember it bein'. Someone, probably Pops, put a new head on the scarecrow, but he never did seem quite as scary as he was before. It was the eyes that made all the difference. The new eyes were smaller and different colors. The thread used to sew them on started off bein' white, but it became all dirty and tattered over time, to the point where one of them eyes fell right off. He still has the one eye now, but I know he sees nothin'. It's not like it was before.

BK: Even years later, they never did find Calvin's body? I'm sorry, I know it's an insensitive question.

Paul: That's a story for someone else to tell. I'm sure you'll be hearin' about it if you decide to stick around. I've said what I had to say, but I'm done now. Anyway, it's almost my turn to sing again. Plus, your next guest looks like she's ready to spill her guts.

BK: What song are you doing this time?

Paul: It's always the same song, don't you know that yet? It's Strawberry Fields Forever for me, always will be.

Dancing Queen by Ursula

BK: Hi there. Please, take a seat.

Ursula: Are you sure you don't mind? I thought perhaps you might need a break, or maybe even a shower after talking to that sexist pig for the last hour.

BK: Um, no, it's all good. He wasn't that bad.

Ursula: I'll bet he had some wonderful things to say about me. I'm being sarcastic, obviously. No-one in this town has ever had anything good to say about me, not even my parents. I'm the girl they talk all about in hushed tones and pray for in church. They should be praying for their own souls. I'm at peace with mine.

BK: Wow. Well, maybe we should ease into this conversation a little before we get to all of that. I'm not sure if you know why I'm talking to you. Can you please start by telling me your name? I'm Brian.

Ursula: I'm Ursula, and yes, I do know why you are here. You want to know all about the songs we sing here and the stories behind them, right?

BK: Yes, that's exactly right, but I also want to know a little about you, too, before you get to the story. Ursula is not a common name in small-town Georgia, I wouldn't think.

Ursula: I don't know about that, but I can tell you how I came by the name. It seems that my ancestors were from Germany. They were escaping some war or another, although I have no idea which one. The subject bores me to tears as it's nothing but small-minded, small-dicked men starting battles to prove how macho they are. We'd never be in a war if women ruled the world. Anyway, being of German descent, I was given a name that was meant to honor my heritage.

BK: You don't seem to be much of a fan of the male species.

Ursula: I'm not the man-hating bitch that I probably sound like right now, and for some strange reason I feel as though I can trust you. I can sense that you are kind. It's just that men have never really been particularly kind to me, especially when they find out that I'm not interested in entertaining their clumsy advances. I understand that my family needed to escape and find somewhere safer to live, but I can't help feeling that their decision to come here set the wheels in motion for the events that would finally happen to me.

BK: I just want to hear your story, Ursula. I have no other agenda outside of that. Can we start with your family? What made them move to this part of the United States?

Ursula: From what I've been told, which is precious little, they were farmers in Germany. They came here with nothing more than the clothes on their back and a desire to work. How they ended up in Redfield appears to be something of a mystery, but they were welcomed in by the small group of families that lived here at the time. Even when they had settled and had the opportunity to move on, they chose to stay. This town has a way of holding you in place and keeping you from wandering too far. I would wager that no-one here has ever ventured across state lines. They all seem content to stay and wallow.

BK: What about you? Have you traveled?

Ursula: I thought I had found my way out of this awful little town, but that opportunity was taken away from me. After everything went down, I felt more alone than ever here, but I didn't have the heart to get away on my own. I don't think I would have made it, if I'm being totally honest. I decided to stay rather than taking the chance to get out, only to return later with my tail tucked between my legs. They would have all loved that, and I wasn't about to give them the satisfaction.

BK: Where would you have gone had you left? Did you have a destination in mind?

Ursula: Definitely. We always talked about heading west and moving to California. It was a bit of a pipe dream, we both knew that. California is a long way from here, plus neither of us had the type of money that you would need to get there, never mind make a home. Still, there was something romantic about the idea of lazing on the beach and soaking up the sun, as well as living in a place where people weren't constantly judging you for your sexuality. We would get stares all the time here. We didn't even have to be holding hands or showing outward signs of affection to feel those glares. We just had to be together. That was enough to get the hate stew simmering in this town.

BK: I'm sorry you had to go through that. I grew up in a small town in Alabama, and I know how folks can get when someone in the community is even just a little different. I want to hear more about your early life here, but I ultimately want to know about your song choice. Is Dancing Queen a song that you personally relate to, or does it remind you of someone else in your life?

Ursula: It reminds me of Tina. I can see her as clear as day when I sing. It hurts to have her so close but not be able to reach out and touch her. It's like having the most amazing dream ever, only to wake up and realize your life is as miserable as it was the moment you closed your eyes the night before.

BK: If it hurts so much, why sing that song?

Ursula: I can't explain it. I need to, it's that simple.

BK: I think I understand. Tina must have had quite the impact on your life. Can you talk to me about her?

Ursula: Her influence will probably make more sense if I tell you a little about my life before she came into it. Is that okay with you?

BK: Of course, please.

Ursula: As I said earlier, my family has lived here almost from the day that the town of Redfield was founded. Paul's family was the first to settle here. No-one knows for sure if they planted the strawberry fields or whether they just happened to stumble upon them and claim them as their own. My guess would be the latter given the nature of that truly rotten family. Since my relatives were farmers, it made sense for them to settle here and help turn the strawberry patch into a bigger business. From what I know, they lived with Paul's parents until they were able to build a home of their own. There were a few other families already here at that point, and they all helped with the construction of what became our little slice of property heaven.

BK: How many families were there in the early days of Redfield?

Ursula: It was a small community. Probably only ten or eleven back in those days. They were obviously not a particularly imaginative bunch. I mean, is Redfield the best name they could come up with for this place? It's as though one of them looked out the window, saw the strawberry fields and had a eureka moment. Dullards, the lot of them. This place was nothing but strawberries and dirt roads, yet they were all so protective of it. I once saw my mom pull out a shotgun and chase a salesman off our front porch. Unless you were here to work or buy fruit, you were not welcome. At least that was the way it was back in the early days. Not that we get many visitors now. You are a very welcome sight, since I can't remember the last time a stranger walked into this bar. It might even have been Tina who was the last one.

BK: So, Tina was not a resident of Redfield?

Ursula: No. She was from Atlanta, born and raised. She was so beautiful; stuck out like a sore thumb in this hick town. She never did tell me what brought her here originally, although there is a very good chance that I never asked. I was so in awe of her that I just assumed God sent her. Yes, I know that sounds about as corny as it gets, but she was like an angel to me. I had spent so much of my time to that point trying to be invisible that I couldn't believe she saw me.

BK: Why the need to be invisible?

Ursula: I already told you. Everyone in this town knew what I was, but it didn't stop every guy trying to get inside my pants. Listen, I know I don't have much to offer in the looks department. If you were to Google "German farm girl," you might just come across a picture of me. I was always bigger than other girls, and I was never interested in trying to make myself look pretty. Being a big girl meant getting boobs, and as soon as they popped out, the guys started paying attention. There's not a lot of women to go around in this town, so looks weren't considered to be a high priority on the lists of horny farm workers.

Even before I knew what being gay meant, I knew I was different. All of the girls my age would talk about how yucky boys were, but they all reached a point where those words were not quite as believable. They would start wearing tighter clothes, splash on some make-up, and talk about the guys they couldn't stand, all while getting a little flushed at the idea of seeing those boys the very next day. I saw my friends the same way that all the guys in town did. Those tiny little shorts and the smell of their soaps and perfumes would make my heart race. I made the mistake of telling my feelings to someone who I believed was my best friend. She was disgusted and couldn't wait to let everyone else know. The girls all shunned me at the same time the boys were making bets as to which one of them could convert me.

BK: That must have been a truly awful time for you.

Ursula: Initially, yes, but I grew a thick skin quite quickly. The more I ignored their taunts, the less they bothered me. I took to wearing coveralls and big plaid shirts that covered the few decent curves that I had. The last guy who tried to make a move on me ended up with a broken nose. By that time, I was picking up a few shifts at a bar just outside town. A bunch of guys from Redfield came in, and I could see them laughing and pointing at me all night. I had taken a quick bathroom break, and when I came out, one of them was blocking the hallway back into the bar. The rest of them were at the end of the passageway making sure that no-one else got through.

Anyway, the guy blocking my way decided that it might be a good idea to greet me with his pathetic little dick sticking out of his pants. He grabbed my hand and tried to force it down between his legs, but he made the mistake of grabbing my right hand. I am a leftie, and I socked him good. It hurt like hell, but the crunching noise that his nose made when I busted it made me feel a whole lot better. He ran off screaming, his stubby little pecker still out for all the world to see. I charged after him, yelling that I was going to kill him or anyone else who ever dared put their hands on me again. That was the night that the taunting stopped and the whispering began. They all still saw me, but I finally felt that I had achieved the invisibility I so desired.

BK: You might have become my new hero. That was incredibly brave.

Ursula: I don't know about that. I felt quite stupid right after it. I was essentially an outsider in my hometown, and I've already told you that outsiders were not looked upon very kindly. It could all have gone bad very quickly for me, but they all chose to leave me alone after that incident, probably thinking I was a little mad. I mean, I fight boys and fuck girls, neither of which are things you would expect from a sane southern belle.

BK: You seem perfectly sane to me, Ursula. That said, I do believe I am a little more open-minded than the people you are describing. Can you talk to me about Tina now? I want to know how you two met and how she changed your life.

Ursula: After I hit that guy, things got pretty quiet at the bar, for me at least. Life went on there as normal, which meant that no-one was paying any attention to me at all. I was fine with that. All I wanted to do was go in, serve some drinks, make a little money, and then go home. That's exactly what happened for a few weeks after the fight, but then one night the bar was way busier than usual. It was a

KARAOKE NIGHT

Friday night. We always drew a decent crowd on the weekend, but the place was jumping this particular Friday.

It was busy, but there was none of the usual trouble that we sometimes see on payday nights. Everyone seemed intent on having a good time, and that prompted the bar manager to turn up the sound system to create an even bigger party atmosphere. In one corner of the bar, there was an old dance floor that was nothing more than a waste of space. No-one ever got up to dance, and it ended up being more like a boxing ring, as that was where drunk guys would go to throw down, or throw up, whichever came first. I was constantly having to mop up blood stains in that area, plus we had a little jar behind the bar where we kept the teeth that would come out in those fights.

BK: Wait, what?

Ursula: Oh yeah, there was quite the collection there. The tooth fairy would have been bankrupt if she had ever come across that jar. So, the music is going, and everyone is having a great time, right up until the moment an Abba song comes on. To that point, it had been nothing but old country tunes and southern rock, so it was a little jarring to hear Dancing Queen come on right after listening to the Allman Brothers and Lynyrd Skynyrd for a couple of hours straight.

The guys who came into our bar were rough and ready types, and you can bet that not one of them wanted to be caught dead out on the dance floor when Abba came on. They bolted out of there, parting the dance floor like the Red Sea, and there she was. Have you ever seen videos of Stevie Nicks back in the day when she was singing with Fleetwood Mac?

BK: Sure.

Ursula: That's what she was like. She looked like an angel, spinning to the music as though she was suspended in mid-air. It was the most beautiful thing I had ever seen in my life. I couldn't take my eyes off her. It was more than just her looks; it was the way she seemed to shimmer and give off her own light. It probably sounds to you as though I am making her seem more than she really was, but I'm telling you, she was this ethereal presence that seemed at odds with a place as scummy as that bar was.

I remember that the bar went pretty quiet for a minute, yet no-one was paying any attention to Tina out on the floor. It was as if they were consciously trying not to make eye contact with her, but rather than talking to cover for their discomfort, they were all just staring off into space. I couldn't stop looking at her, though. I felt truly alive for the first time in my life as if I had finally just plugged myself into some wonderful life force that filled me with happiness. When she finally looked at me, I felt sure I was going to explode.

BK: What did you do?

Ursula: Nothing, nothing at all. I just stood there staring at her with my mouth hanging open. I snapped out of it a little when the song ended, but I was sucked right back in when Dancing Queen started playing again. That song being on repeat seemed to break the hold that Tina had on the place. I clearly remember someone loudly yelling "FUCK" before yanking the jukebox plug right out of the wall. As soon as the music went quiet, the party atmosphere returned. The jukebox was turned back on and launched right into a George Strait tune.

BK: What was Tina doing during all of this?

Ursula: Staring at me. I might have been invisible to everyone else in that bar, but she saw me, saw right through to the heart of me. The crowd swallowed her up once they all got back on the dance floor, which seemed to break the spell I was under, but I was trembling. I was holding a couple of glasses, and the beer was spilling all over my hands as I shook. I didn't have anywhere to put them down, so imagine how relieved I was when someone plucked them out of my hands and solved the problem for me. I turned to say thanks, and there she was, standing beside me with the most glorious smile ever painted on her face. I was suddenly speechless, and it felt as though it took me about twenty minutes to tell her my name after she introduced herself. She held my hands and smiled at me, making everything around me disappear. Once my surroundings slipped away, and she was all I could see, I instantly relaxed. We made plans to meet up outside the bar after my shift was over. I knew nothing about Tina except her name, but I instantly trusted her.

BK: Love at first sight?

Ursula: No, it was peace at first sight, although love was a pretty close second. I never realized how troubled and depressed I was until I met Tina and felt all that weight fall away from me. It felt as though I floated across the bar for the rest of the night, and it was almost as time took on the consistency of treacle, slow and sluggish. My shift finally ended though, and there she was waiting for me, just as she had promised.

BK: What did you two do that night, or is it too personal a question?

Ursula: Relax, there are no sordid details to share from that night. There was an all-night diner in the town where the bar was, and that was where we ended up. When it came to talking about our lives, I assumed we were doomed. We may as well have come from two different planets. I was a plain Jane farm girl dyke while she was a lipstick lesbian with a booming career in Atlanta. Like I said earlier, I never did find out how she came to land in my part of the world, but despite our obvious differences, it felt like fate. We were together as often as possible from that night forward.

BK: Tell me a little about that time. What was your life like together?

Ursula: After that first night, I didn't see her again for two weeks, which just happened to be the longest two weeks of my life. She promised me she would be back, but I spent the whole time convincing myself that I'd never see her again. When she walked through the front door of the bar on her second visit,

I very nearly burst into tears. I think I've made it clear that I'm not a girlie-girl, so that little emotional outburst seriously took me by surprise. She walked in, came striding over, and gave me a huge hug which she followed up with a passionate kiss that made me more than a little self-conscious. Everyone knew I was gay, but they certainly weren't used to seeing me flaunt it in a big way. I turned beet red, but as Tina turned to head over to the jukebox, she took a moment to whisper in my ear. Let them look, she said to me, it turns me on. That really set my face afire, but it also filled my entire body with a warm glow that was unlike anything I had ever felt before. There were a lot of firsts during my time with Tina.

I don't know how she managed it, but she was somehow able to get Dancing Queen on the jukebox three or four times that night. There would always be a loud groan when it came on, but no-one ever said a word to her or called her out for killing the redneck vibe in the bar. If truth be told, they all seemed a little wary of Tina, giving her a wide berth. This was stunning to me because she was far and away the hottest girl that had ever set foot in the bar, at least during my time there. She was immaculate from top to bottom: her features, her curves, the way she dressed. She was the complete package, yet not one guy ever tried to make a move on her. It was a little weird.

There was no late-night coffee and conversation that night. I'll spare you all the details, but what I will tell you is that we went back to her hotel room and didn't leave for a full twenty-four hours. It was my first sexual encounter, and I can't imagine that it could have been any more perfect. There hasn't been anyone since Tina, and even if there had been, they could never have reached the bar that she set. I felt visible, but more than that, I felt awakened. I was finally on the path I was supposed to be following, the one that would lead me out of here and away to somewhere blissful.

BK: What was it that took you off that path, Ursula?

Ursula: Something evil, something rotten to the core. The people in this town didn't care for me at all, but they were going to be damned if they would let me leave.

BK: How so?

Ursula: Tina spent the first couple of months of our time together coming here to see me, but she was a busy woman and needed to spend more time at home. She started suggesting that I come and spend some time at her place, knowing that it was going to be a hard sell. I hate it here, but it's all I had ever known. I wanted nothing more than to get out, but I was like a shut-in who sees the world outside the known as something to be mistrusted.

She spent a lot of time telling me about where she lived. While she worked in downtown Atlanta, she had a home in a nearby town called Decatur. She would tell me about all the cool places to eat and drink there, and how gays were welcomed with open arms. It sounded like some kind of utopia to me, which made it harder for me to believe what she was saying. On the other hand, I knew it wasn't fair that she was the one constantly making the effort to be together. I had no vehicle and no easy way to get to the city, but since Tina was offering to come pick me up, I really had no excuse.

BK: So, you finally caved in and made the trip?
Ursula: I did.
BK: How was that for you?
Ursula: It's difficult to put into words how it felt being there for the first time. I still had that feeling of invisibility, but it had more to do with the people around me being so wrapped up in their thing that my existence was really none of their business. They were not consciously avoiding my gaze the way they do here, and they certainly weren't making snide remarks behind my back. It was the first time that my invisibility felt somehow wrong. I suddenly wanted to be seen and to connect with other people, Having Tina by my side was certainly a confidence booster.

BK: Tell me more about your first visit.
Ursula: It was all a bit of a blur if I am being totally honest. I didn't do much during the day while Tina was at work, but in the evenings, we would go eat and drink, hang out with some of her friends, and usually end up in some bar or club having drinks and listening to music. Everyone was so friendly, and they all spoke about how happy Tina had been since meeting me. It was an emotional time, but in a good way, finally.

Anyway, we took to alternating visits between Redfield and Atlanta, but as time passed, we spent more and more time at her place. She was constantly buying me new clothes and other little things, suggesting that I leave them there rather than taking them home. She was well into the process of moving me in before I ever noticed.

BK: Did she eventually ask you to move in with her?

Ursula: She did, but I never got to answer properly. I wish she could have heard me say yes, even just once.

BK: What happened?

Ursula: She arrived in Redfield that night, came to the bar, and told me to give my notice. I remember she had this big goofy grin on her face as she said it. She even suggested that I quit right then and there, but she also knew I would never do that. I asked her what was going on, but she said she wasn't telling me anything until I got off work that night. As was so often the case when Tina was in town, time ground to a standstill in the hours we were unable to be together.

This time, though, she didn't hang around in the bar during my shift, and she didn't dance or play Dancing Queen. She loved getting people riled up in that town, so I figured she must have had something serious up her sleeve if she was avoiding the opportunity to have a little fun.

Tina was outside the bar waiting for me when I left, and she instantly hooked her arm in mine and started skipping down the street with me in tow. I was a little embarrassed, but I skipped right along, such was her way of always being able to pull me out of my shell. We got back to her car, where she told me that we were heading back to my place so that I could pick up all my important things. I begged her to tell me what was going on, but she said it was a secret until all my stuff was in the car. I didn't have a lot to pack, so I was done and loaded in no time, all while begging her to tell me what was going on. She was having a grand old time, teasing me and giggling like a little schoolgirl. Her joy was infectious, and I was soon laughing along with her. I was excited and nervous all at the same time.

BK: Did you have any idea what was going on?

Ursula: My guess was that we were going on a trip. We had talked about having a romantic getaway, but this somehow felt different, although I couldn't explain how. Once everything was loaded, she became really serious. She launched into this wonderful speech about how much she loved me and about how she wanted to spend every waking moment with me. It was then that she said that moving in together seemed the best way to achieve that goal. I was speechless for a moment, but just when I was about to say yes, we heard this strange growling noise.

BK: Like an animal growl?

Ursula: Yes and no. It sounded feral and unhinged, that growl, but it also didn't sound like any animal I had ever heard. We both turned in the direction of the sound and saw what looked like a pair of red eyes staring at us. I was terrified, but Tina was all business. She took me by the arm and started leading me round to the front of the car. The driver's side was by the sidewalk, so getting me to the passenger seat meant stepping out onto the road. As soon as we hit the street, the growling got louder and the red eyes just kept getting bigger and bigger. It took a moment for it to sink in that it was a car, one of those big muscle cars from the seventies. It was bright red in color, and the headlights had a weird red ring around them.

BK: Halo lights.

Ursula: Is that what they're called? Anyway, it made the headlights look totally red and awfully menacing. Tina was pulling at my arm, but I just stood rooted to the spot. I was hypnotized by those lights, even though I knew I was about to be swallowed whole by that beast of a car. Just as it was almost upon us, Tina stopped pulling and pushed me instead. I felt the breeze blow through my hair as the car flew past, but it was the sounds that I will never forget.

My back was to the car when I hit the ground, so I didn't see the impact, but you better believe that I heard it. There was this weird muffled thump when it hit her, but the thing that stands out from that moment was the sound Tina made. It was a whooshing sound, as though all the air was sucked out of her during the collision. By the time I turned around, she had gone airborne; her head connected with the top of the windshield, sending her spinning. It would have been graceful were it not so awful. It was all happening in slow motion now, and I remember having time to think that she was going to split her skull wide open on the pavement. That didn't happen. She went through another half spin, landing on her feet, the impact snapping her ankles. I heard her bones breaking, I heard it. That sound brought me back and made time seem real again.

BK: Jesus. Did you see the driver?

Ursula: No. The windows were jet black. All they did was send out the reflection of the streetlights. There were no plates either, just a space where they should have been. When I got to Tina, she was a mess. You could see the bone peeking through the gash in her forehead, her legs were bent every which way, and her breathing was really shallow. Someone must have saw what happened because I started hearing sirens right away and the paramedics were there in minutes. They worked on her there, but they eventually called in a life flight ambulance, saying they needed to get her to Atlanta if she was to have any shot at living.

BK: Did you go with her?

Ursula: They wouldn't let me. They took her away, and I never saw her alive again. They did manage to save her life, and they had her on a ventilator for a couple of days. I called all her friends in the city and begged them all to come and get me. Two of them promised to come for me, as their plan was to pick up her car and take it back.

I picked up a shift at the bar on the day they were coming. It seemed to me to be a better idea than just waiting around fretting. It was a quiet day at the bar. Hardly anyone was in, and the people who were in weren't saying much. From out of nowhere, Dancing Queen comes on the jukebox. I look over to the dance floor, and there she is, just the way I saw her on that first night. This time, though, she really was spinning in mid-air. Slowly but surely, she turned in my direction and blew me a kiss. Everything was fuzzy and out of focus because I was crying and basically losing my shit. It all snapped back into focus when the bar manager touched my arm and asked if I was okay. The music was gone and so was Tina, just like that.

Her friends came as promised that night, but as soon as I saw them, I knew she had passed. We cried together and spoke about how much we loved Tina. I told them that I wouldn't be going to the funeral. They were surprised, and maybe even a little angry, but how could I possibly explain to them that I wanted to remember her the way I had seen her in the bar that day, positively glowing and ever so full of life?

BK: I am so sorry for your loss, Ursula. Did they ever find the car or the driver?

Ursula: I doubt they'll ever find the driver, but there is a story about the car, which I think you are about to hear now. Hey Neil, it's your turn.

Barracuda by Neil

Authors note: This was the one interview where I had to get the most creative. Neil was not a very talkative man and what I did get out of him was tough to decipher due to him having one of the most severe stutters I have ever heard. I did not include it in the text, but I should note that in the original recording, Neil claims that the stutter only appeared after the events described in the interview.

BK: Please, come have a seat. It's Neil, right?

Neil: Yes. Yes, that's me. Neil.

BK: It's a pleasure to meet you, Neil. Ursula tells me you might know something about the hit and run involving her girlfriend.

Neil: I don't know who did it, if that if that's what you are asking.

BK: Sorry, no. She said you might know something about the vehicle that was involved.

Neil: Um, yes, yes, that's something I know about for sure.

BK: Great. Ursula didn't really go into any detail about what you might know. Can you fill me in on some of the details? My guess, judging by how things are going so far, is that the vehicle in question was a Plymouth Barracuda. Is that right?

Neil: Yes, yes, a flame-red Barracuda. It was a 1973 model, one of the last years they made them. It was, she was probably the most beautiful car I have ever set eyes on. She almost glowed and didn't have a mark on her when I got my hands on her. That was, that was a little surprising given that she had been used in a hit and run.

BK: How did…

Neil: Before we get into all this, I need to ask you a question. Did she, did Ursula tell you about the night she socked that dude at the bar?

BK: Yes, she did. Were you the guy she hit, Neil?

Neil: What? No. No, but I was there. I was one of the guys who blocked the path in and out. I didn't, I wanted no part of it, but I was there with a bunch of guys from work. They were constantly picking on me, and I thought I might get on their good side and get them, get them all off my back a little if I played along. I had nothing against Ursula and her friend. They never did me any harm, so I had no, I didn't have a grievance with either of them. After I saw what went down, I apologized to Ursula for my part in all of it. She was, Ursula was cool about it, probably because I was probably the only guy in Redfield who never tried to make a move on her. Thing is, the thing is that word got back to the guys at work about my apology, and they rode, and they were even harder on me from that point forward.

BK: Where did you work?

Neil: It was, I worked in the scrapyard. It was mostly old cars that we took in. If they were in decent shape, we would let folks come in and pick working parts. The cars that were trashed would get crushed and shipped out. Funnily, funnily enough, it was mostly cars that were broken down and abandoned that we got. Quite often, I could tinker with them and get them going again. The manager, the boss would take those cars and re-sell them, give me a little slice of the profits.

BK: Were you a trained mechanic?

Neil: No. No, but it was what I always wanted to be. When I, back when I was younger, I loved to mess around with old things to see how they worked. My dad was a bit of a collector of junk and would often pick up old radios and clocks and stuff and bring them home. It would drive my mom nuts because all that old junk would get piled up in the garage, with my dad promising to fix it or sell it at some point. He never, he didn't ever get around to it though, and the pile just got bigger and bigger. I got, I started digging around in that stuff to find things to play with, and I remember coming across this cool old clock. It was a table clock that sat inside a glass dome, and it had a little device, like three brass balls on a column, on the bottom that was supposed to spin when the clock was working. I started messing with the insides of that clock, and before long I had it working. My mom loved it and put it on the shelf over the fireplace, which was where it stayed until, until the day she passed.

BK: Did you fix other stuff too?

Neil: Oh, yeah. I fixed, I fixed all sorts of different things. It just seemed to come to me naturally. Once I looked at the internal workings, my brain could figure out how it was all supposed to go.

From there, it became, it was easy to settle on the problem and get it fixed. Clocks and watches were the easiest to repair, but I soon moved on to radios and some other stuff. My dad would see me repair all those things and got the idea to start selling them. He told me, he said that he would take what he called a finder's fee and that he would put the rest of the money away for me. He said it was my college fund. It may not have seemed like much, but that, but his idea put a little fire under me. I studied hard at school and got my grades up real quick. It was, it was as though the smarter I got at school, the easier it became to fix all the junk that my dad would bring home. It wasn't until I fixed his truck that I really got the idea, that I started to think about being a mechanic.

BK: So, did you manage to save enough for college, or at least for trade school?

Neil: I don't, I never did find out. My dad took off when I was in high school. Mom, my mom said that he had taken all that money he had stashed away for me and used it to set himself and his fancy piece up in a nice place somewhere in Texas. I didn't, I mean I never thought to ask how much I was making all that time. Whenever I brought it up, dad would slip me a few bucks and tell me to go see a movie or something. He was my dad, so it didn't really occur to me that he might be messing with my money.

BK: How long ago did he leave, and did you ever hear from him?

Neil: It was years ago now. I've never, he never got in touch with me after that, and since he wasn't making an effort, I didn't see why I should bother either. By that time, by then, word was out that I was a regular fixer-upper, so I made myself a few dollars here and there, but never enough to even think about going to college. Besides, besides my mom needed some help with the bills, so most of my fix-it money went towards that.

BK: How did you end up landing the job at the scrapyard?

Neil: That was, that was through a friend of my mum's, Mr. Bryce. I think they might have had more going on, but whatever the case, he took, he took a real shine to me. Whenever he stopped by the house, which was a lot, he would drop off items that he referred to as pet projects. It seems, it seems as though he had heard about my knack for fixing things, so he wanted to put it to the test. I was never able to fix everything I got my hands on, but, but I guess I did enough, as he gave me a job on the day I finished high school.

There were, he had five other guys working then when I started, so there really wasn't a lot of money to go around, which meant I was on the low end of the totem pole when it came to payday. Still, Mr. Bryce was always very kind to me, which is what I think got the other guys going against me from the start. It got even worse when they learned that I had started making extra money from the fixing and re-selling deal. A couple of them tried to get in on the action, but they, but they were never any good at getting the junkers up and running.

BK: How would they pick on you?

Neil: It was, they would call me names and play practical jokes on me all the time. I became known as Bryce's bitch around the workplace, but I would just laugh them off and try to ignore them. Craig Black and Alan Garland were the worst, as they were the ringleaders. The other three guys just sort of played along, but they really weren't so bad. If you, if you got any of those three on their own, they were always friendly enough. It was the group mentality thing that made them play along; plus, they were all a little scared of Craig. Turned, it turned out that they were right to be, but I'm sure someone else will tell you all about his antics.

BK: Noted. Can you jump ahead to your story about the Barracuda?

Neil: Yes, yes I can. By the time she landed in the scrapyard, things had turned really sour. It was Craig who had been smacked by Ursula, and he was not well pleased about my apologizing to her. He went, he went out of his way to pick on me after that. The practical jokes became a little less jokey and a little more intimidating, to the point where a couple of the other guys started to spend less and less time around him. Not, not Ian, though. Those two remained thick as thieves.

It was almost a month after the hit and run that the Barracuda showed up in our yard. Like I, like I said before, she was in pristine condition. The police had gone over her with a fine tooth comb but never came up with any prints or anything that they could use as evidence against whoever was behind the wheel that night. If I had thought Craig could have gotten his hands on a car like that, I would not have been surprised to hear that he had gone after that poor girl, but I also knew he wouldn't be, wouldn't be smart enough not to leave any evidence behind.

BK: How did everyone react to the vehicle being dropped off?

Neil: We, we were all a little surprised, to be honest. I guess we all thought that it would end up in the impound until someone claimed it, which no-one was ever going to do. The cop who was there when it was dropped off told us that the guys at the impound lot demanded that it be taken away, said they were having nightmares and seeing things that shouldn't rightly exist. Mr. Bryce told the cop that he would take care of it, but he called me into the office shortly after to let me in on his real plan.

He, Mr. Bryce didn't like the idea of crushing that Barracuda without first making some money off it. He knew that he couldn't sell it as is, but he, but he thought he could make a killing selling all the engine parts individually. He asked, he asked me if I would be willing to break it all down before it went in the crusher, quoting a ridiculous sum of money for the job. I didn't feel quite right about doing it, but the money he was offering, along with what I had saved, would be enough to get me into trade school. I agreed, I decided that I would do it, but he suggested that I sleep in the break room while I was working on it, as he didn't want the other guys to know what was going on. He said, he said he would make up some story to explain why I was staying there, just in case any of the guys caught wind that I was bunking down at the yard.

BK: What did he end up telling them?

Neil: He told, he told them that my mom was really sick and that what she had was contagious. He said that he couldn't risk me losing any time at work given how busy things were, so that was why I was staying in the break room. None of the guys said anything in front of the boss, but the Bryce's bitch name calling reached fever pitch for a few days.

That first night, things went off without much of a hitch. It was, it was tough breaking her down with not much light to work with, but I made good time and had some parts ready to go the next day. It was the second night when things started to get weird.

BK: Weird in what way?

Neil: The window, the window in the break room looked out over the yard, and a couple of times that second night I woke up with everything bathed in red. By the time I got up and got to the window, everything was black again, but I swear I saw the halo lights on the Barracuda glowing a little. I thought, I thought it was just a trick of the light, but it gave me the creeps. The next night, there was growling to go with that red light. One of the guys heard me telling Mr. Bryce about what I was seeing and how I thought it was coming from the car. They stopped, they stopped calling me Bryce's bitch at that point, calling me Christine instead, like the, like the car in that Stephen King book.

I worked on that car two more nights and damn near, damn near reached my breaking point. I had removed the halo lights by then, but that thing kept on growling through the night, keeping me awake and afraid. I heard the lock rattling on the door to the main building a few times and what sounded like people whispering right in my ear.

BK: What were the voices saying?

Neil: I'm, I'm not entirely sure, but it sounded like they were saying 'bone daddy' over and over again. It could be my mind playing tricks, though, given what I found that last night.

BK: What was it?

Neil: It was, it was a big old piece of bone wedged right into the upper radiator hose. I heard that girl's legs were all messed up when she was hit, so I don't know if it came from her or if someone got wind of what I was up to and put it in there to mess with me. Either way, I gave it to Mr. Bryce and he said he would take care of it. He paid me the money he promised me right there and then and told me that we would be crushing the car in a couple of days.

It was, it was Craig Black who was in charge of working the crusher, and he seemed disappointed that we were finally going to put the girl to rest. He kept going on about how the car was serving God by killing queers, as well as a whole bunch of other hateful talk. Alan hadn't shown up for work on the day of the crushing, and Craig wanted to wait, but Mr. Bryce insisted. I believe, I believe that the boss started feeling the heavy sensation that had fallen over the yard since the Barracuda arrived. It seemed to get thicker and harder to breathe with each passing day.

When he, when Craig was loading up the crusher with the car, I could hear him singing over the sound of the machinery. It was that same song that the girl used to play at the bar. I was going, going to say something to him when I heard the screaming start. It was, it was coming from inside the Barracuda. The windows were black as pitch, but the passenger window was open enough where we could see inside just enough to know that Alan was in there. He was, he was swinging an empty bottle of Jack Daniels at the window, trying to break it as he screamed at us to stop the crusher. Craig mashed down on the emergency stop button over and over, but the, but the crusher kept right on going.

BK: Good sweet Jesus.

Neil: That machine, that crusher was a slow mover. I seemed to take forever to put a dent in the roof of the car. As soon, as soon as it did, the windows all shattered. When they broke, Alan started to try and climb out, but it looked as though he, he got caught up in the seat-belt. I'm not, I'm not going to lie to you, it looked to me as though that belt was tugging him back in as opposed to simply holding him in place. He had just got his neck and shoulders out when the crusher finally caught up to him. Pieces of gore went flying this way and that, and while it may just have been an echo in my ears, it sounded like he was screaming all the way as his head fell to the ground.

I stayed on a little while longer after that, mostly because most of the other guys up and quit. Craig stayed on, but he, but he didn't say much. I think something snapped inside him that day, although it took a little while longer for him to go right off the deep end. The scrapyard eventually closed down, but I was long gone by then. I finally became a, a fully qualified mechanic, just like I had always wanted. There are still some nights when I wake up and see red. I can, can hear the growls and whispers in my room, but they all vanish as soon as I switch on the bedside lamp. I don't think that Barracuda is finished with me, and I know I'll never be finished with her.

BK: What about…

Neil: Sorry, sir. No more, no more questions. My time is up. You have someone else waiting for you now.

Bad to the Bone by Ian

BK: That's one of my favorite songs you were singing just then.

Ian: Well, doesn't that just fill my heart with fucking joy, making you so very happy. There is nothing to enjoy about that song.

BK: Yet, here you are doing it.

Ian: What fucking choice do I have? You tell me, man.

BK: I'm not sure what to say to that, but I do think we got off on the wrong foot. My name is Brian Keane, and I am a blogger interested in learning more about this town, but specifically about the songs being sung. And you are?

Ian: Ian Bryce.

BK: Are you in any way related to the Mr. Bryce that Neil was just talking about. The gentleman who owned the scrapyard?

Ian: Ha-ha. Gentleman? You are fucking joking, right? Having a laugh at my expense, are you? Well, fuck you and fuck all the rest of them in this place. None of you know anything about that miserable fuck.

BK: Then why not use this as your opportunity to tell your side of the story? I'm assuming that "Bad to the Bone" makes you think of your father, am I right?

Ian: It does, but probably not in the way that you are thinking. Yes, he was a bad motherfucker, but there's more to it than that. He was, from what I was witness to, totally fucking evil.

BK: Tell me, Ian. It sounds to me like you are the victim here, but I can't really be sure until I get the whole picture. From what Neil told me, your father sounded like a pretty decent man.

Ian: He went out of his way to make everyone think that he was the salt of the fucking earth. It was when he was around the people that should have mattered to him, by which I mean me and my fucking mom, that the very worst came out in him. He was bitter and angry all the time and given that he spent the whole fucking day hiding it, his true nature would come pouring out in ways you wouldn't even imagine when he walked over the welcome mat and into the family home.

BK: He was abusive?

Ian: Fuck, yes, he was abusive, but it was the thought that must have gone into those abuses that was the scary thing. He didn't really drink, so you can't even blame the booze for his appalling fucking behavior. He was just rotten to the core, yet you won't find a single person outside of me and my mom, God rest her fucking soul, who will ever say anything bad about him. Fuck, stuttering Neil there probably believes that the sun rose and set in and out of dad's asshole.

The really scary thing was that he didn't have a trigger. The house was always kept immaculate by my mom, dinner was always on the table, and I was always respectful and polite, yet none of that stopped him from going off. He couldn't wait to get home and just lay the fuck into both of us. I got it bad, but I know mom got it worse. There were nights when I couldn't sleep, and I could hear muffled screams coming from down in the cellar. He at least had the common fucking decency to wait until I turned 13 before he introduced me to the shit show that he had created down in that cellar, but I spent years wondering what was down there and what he was doing to my mom.

BK: What was down there?

Ian: Have you ever seen one of those medieval movies where the king has a torture chamber used to fuck with people who didn't kiss his ass?

BK: Yes.

Ian: It was like that, only way more over the fucking top. He kept all his hunting gear down there, but he also made a solid fucking collection of torture toys that he loved to test out on mom and me.

BK: Wait a minute. You said he made them?

Ian: Oh yeah, he was a regular fucking handyman. Made that Jigsaw dude look like an arts and crafts teaching pussy. I count myself lucky that I only ever got to see a few of those things in action, but that was more than enough for me to figure out that my dad was out of his fucking mind. I know he used to take some things to Neil to fix, although I'm also pretty sure that stuttering fuck didn't have any idea what it was he was actually fixing or making work.

BK: I'm not sure I really want to know, but what did these devices do?

Ian: I can only talk about the one that he used on me, but I can sure as shit guess what some of them were for. Those would be the ones that he saved for my mom. They were shaped like dicks, but they were fucking huge. I never saw a mark on my mom, but there were days when she would be walking around real slow and stooped over. She would always smile and say she was fine, would tell me that she was having women's problems. She was probably all fucking torn up inside given the state of those devices. They were often caked in what looked like dried blood and shit. If I got a little too loud when he was working me over, he would pick up one of those bad boys and wave it in front of my face. The idea of one of those things jammed up my shitter was enough to shut me up and keep me in line.

BK: I'm sorry. I get the idea. You don't need to go into detail about what he did to you.

Ian: Well, bless your heart, aren't you just the sweetest fucking thing. Listen to me, man, if you want to get my story, you don't get to pick and choose what you get to hear. I'm not here to make you comfortable, so just make sure that you keep on listening and recording because I'm only telling you this once. I hear and see this shit in my head every single goddamn fucking day, so you'll excuse me if I want to jump on the opportunity to spill all this shit out in a venue outside of my own fucking skull.

BK: Understood. Go ahead.

Ian: I'm not really sure when he started fucking with me. It could have been from the day that I was born, but the first real memory I have of shit not being right was when I was about 6. We lived in the country, so it was always fucking dark at night, but your eyes would adjust. Even when I had to get up in the middle of the night to go for a piss, you could make out enough to find your way to the toilet and back. Putting on a light when you were supposed to be in bed was a cardinal fucking sin in my house, so you just made do with the dark and the shadows.

I remember one night when I had the shits real bad and was scared that I was going to make a fucking mess all over myself. I jumped out of bed, flicked on that light, and bolted for the toilet. I remember coming back out, and he was right there, screaming in my face and demanding to know why I was spending his fucking money on electricity that I damn sure didn't need. I was sobbing and apologizing, saying it wouldn't happen again, and all that he said in return was that he would show me what true darkness looked like.

I went back to bed, terrified that he was going to hurt me, but nothing else happened that night. My stomach hurt like a bitch when I woke up that next morning, as I had spent the rest of that night with my asshole puckered tight. I was not going to risk getting up and getting another reaming or something worse. It wasn't until about two weeks later that I found out what the fuck he was talking about. I had just about put the memory of the toilet night out of my mind when it all came rushing back in a real hurry.

BK: What did he do to you?

Ian: I remember my mom being really nervous and jumpy all day. She kept fussing over me and being a whole lot more attentive than usual. She was a good mom and always paid me a lot of attention, but she was taking it to another level that day. By the time dad got home, she was about out of her mind. She never showed him any affection, but she was on him the moment he came in the door, loving on him and making sure that all his needs were attended to. She has his favorite fucking dinner made and a glass of good whiskey waiting for him when he got in. Dad just kept brushing her off and asking what had gotten into her, all the while looking over her shoulder at me with a little smirk on his face.

He ate his dinner, drank his whiskey, and pulled my mom to the bedroom, telling me it was time to get to bed. I knew better than to argue, so I went to my room and hunkered down for the night, listening to the old man pounding my mom for what seemed like an eternity. It eventually went quiet enough for me to relax and fall asleep. I don't know how long I was out, but when I opened my eyes, the room was pitch fucking black and I couldn't breathe. I also couldn't fucking move, and I realized that was because my dad was on top of me with a pillow over my face. He would get me to a point where I thought I was going to die before he pulled the pillow away long enough for me to gulp in some fucking air before putting that pillow back on me again. I was in total fucking panic, but he seemed positively giddy. He kept singing that line from a Simon and Garfunkel song, the one that goes "hello darkness my old friend" over and over again. No emotion in his voice, just that same fucking line.

BK: Did you talk to your mom about what was going on?

Ian: I'm sure she already knew. What the fuck could she do? She was getting it worse than I was, at least at that time. She would have loved to have gotten us out of there, but my dad controlled the money and played mom and me against one another. He told me that he would kill her if I ever said a word, so I assume he made similar promises to her. I prayed for him to die every single fucking day of my life. I finally got my prayer answered, but not before he sank deeper into some seriously fucked up shit.

BK: What do you mean?

Ian: He fucked with me at least once a week after the smothering incident. Sometimes it was just little fucking head games that he would play with me, which usually involved going into some serious detail about the things that he was going to do to mom. Other times he would physically fuck with me too. He would tell my mom what he wanted for dinner before he left the house each morning, very often choosing things that he knew I fucking hated. He would stare at me while I ate, taking some perverted joy seeing me trying to get done some awful fucking vegetable or piece of shit meat that he had killed during a hunt. Squirrels, rats, and fuck knows what else were part of my daily meals. If I complained, he would shovel a forkful of food into my face, cover my fucking mouth with his hand, and pinch my nose. Have you ever tried to swallow when you can't fucking breathe? It should be impossible, but I found a way to do it. When I was about 13, I made the mistake of throwing up during one of those dinner sessions. That was when I was introduced to the cellar and his fucked-up bag of tricks.

BK: Can you tell me a bit about what was down there?

Ian: The door down into the cellar always had this huge fucking padlock on it, the key for which was always in his pocket. That night, the one when I threw up, he grabbed a handful of my hair and dragged me to the cellar door. The pain was fucking excruciating, and it was all I could do not to throw up another load of whatever mystery fucking meat he had shoveled into me that night. When we got to the door, he took off his belt and tied it around my neck, pulling me downstairs as though I was a dog on a leash. You had to stoop to get down those stairs, and I remember he bumped his head against the light bulb on the way down. I was struggling a little but started to put up an even bigger fight when the swinging light started to reach deep into the cellar proper.

I had seen some of the devices that he had made, as well as all his hunting gear, but I did not know that he had a fucking surgical table set up down there. There were weird symbols painted all over the walls and a bookshelf filled with all kinds of weird ass titles, many of which were in Latin and other languages that were foreign to me. The spines that I could read and understand were mostly about the occult, black magic, and a ton of other creepy fucking shit. As he dragged me down those stairs and onto the surgical table, I remember thinking that I was about to die.

BK: Good God. How do you deal with that, especially when you are just a kid?

Ian: Honestly, it was thinking that I was going to die that helped me calm the fuck down. I felt totally at peace and was ready to move on. My only worry was that he was going to take his sweet ass time getting the job done. I was all for dying, but I was not about enduring a shitload of pain in order to get there. I should have known he wouldn't kill me though, as that would mean having to give up one of his playthings.

BK: What did he do to you that night?

Ian: He wasn't as cruel as I thought he was going to be. He spent a lot of time talking about his devices and his hunting trips. He told me about casting spells and how they helped him become a great hunter. Spoke about how thankful I should be for his practice of the dark arts. Yes, that's what he called it, the dark fucking arts. He said I should be thankful because we would never go hungry and would always have as much meat as we needed to live. I think he forgot that I had just fucking barfed up his last great catch.

As he was talking, I saw him fiddling with what looked to be a modified drill. This was before the days when you could get the drills with all the interchangeable bits and pieces, so it was a little odd to see him hooking this thing up to what looked like a mini fucking bone saw. Once he had that bit attached, he went a little quiet as he tested it. It was the silence that was the worst, as it made that little fucking drill sound all the more menacing. I would rather have listened to that, though, than have to live through what he did next.

He had me strapped to the table, my hands and feet cuffed like they do with the crazy folks at the looney bin. He took that bone saw contraption and ever so fucking gently nicked the skin right under each of my fingernails. They were the tiniest little cuts, and they barely bled at all, but the pain was fucking intense. I was sobbing and could barely catch my breath. He told me to settle the fuck down, or he would do my feet too, so I pulled my shit together as best I could at that point. Once I had calmed down, he pulled out a Mason jar filled with some Vaseline looking shit, rubbing it on the ends of my fingers. He told me he had made it himself and that it would heal all sorts of injuries. It smelled like ass, but I'll be damned if it didn't work. He told me then that he was trying to make it even better, which meant that more tests would be coming and that me and my mom should be proud to be his little fucking guinea pigs.

BK: Do you need to take a break? We can continue this conversation later if need be.

Ian: Do I look like I need a fucking break? I lived through years of his torturous shit, so I can almost certainly live through talking about it. He fucked with me in the worst possible way, but rather than messing me up, it made me a whole lot stronger. I was going to kill him, but he beat me to it by going and getting himself done in while out hunting.

BK: Tell me about that, about his death.

Ian: When we had out little father/son bonding sessions down in the cellar, he would talk to me about the crazy shit he was up to as he was fucking with me. Some nights, he would use his tools to inflict all manner of wounds on my body, always healing them with his magical fucking salve. Other nights, he would go to town and beat the fuck out of me, sometimes with tools, other times with just his bare hands. Through it all, though, he would always talk crazy shit. Near the end, he started making his own bullets down in the cellar. He would grind down animal bones and mix in dust with the gunpowder, always after he had said a spell over those bones. It sounded as though he was speaking in tongues when he was babbling that fucking nonsense, but he told me that the bullets would become more powerful when they contained the spirit of an animal that he had slaughtered.

BK: I've never heard anything like that. He was truly insane.

Ian: You'd fucking think so, right, yet he was able to hold his shit together when he was running his business and dealing with the general public. Our family had been in Redfield from the very beginning, so that, combined with his general good nature, made him a bit of a beloved character here. Just one more reason why my mom and I could never say a word. The people in this town would never have fucking believed us.

I was about 16 years old when I started to play along with his bullshit. I told him that I wanted to spend more time with him, so I asked for a job at the scrapyard. He seemed pleased with my request, but he also said that working there was below me and that he had bigger fucking ideas for me. I then told him that if I couldn't be part of that family business, then maybe I could help him with the other one, which was the creation of the devices and that fucking healing cream he was making. It was the only time I ever saw him cry when I said that. He fell to his knees, sobbing and chanting some weird fucking tune. He stayed down for quite some time, during which I stayed strapped to the table. When he finally stood up, he looked very unsteady on his feet, but he maintained his shit long enough to tear open my shirt and carve an upside down cross on my chest. It wasn't a deep cut and really didn't hurt, but he licked up the blood that oozed out of the wound before rubbing on his healing cream. Two days later, you would never have known I'd been cut.

BK: How did he behave after that?

Ian: He became a little less rough on me, but that didn't mean that the cellar visits ground to a complete halt. If I left stuff on my plate at dinner, he would let that shit slide, choosing instead to hit my mom and blame her for making food that wasn't good enough for her son to eat. When he started with that, I knew I was going to fucking kill him. I just had to earn his trust first. More and more often I was able to distract him by asking questions about his tools and his fucked-up belief system, the latter of which he seemed to have mashed together by taking chunks out of all those weird books is his collection and creating a bad juju jambalaya. He finally reached a point where he trusted me enough to lay out his entire fucking story and let me tell you, it was a doozie.

BK: What did he tell you?

Ian: He admitted that he was trying to work up the courage to kill either mom or me, but that he had so far failed because he was weak. When I asked him why the fuck he would want to kill his family, he started talking about a giant fucking goat that lived in our little part of the world. This was no ordinary goat, mind you. My dad said that its heart was the source of all the power in the world and that the person who killed the goat and ate the heart would come into possession of that power. The problem was that it had to be killed using a human bone, which is easier said than done when you consider that this big fucking beast had horns as sharp and powerful as it gets. My dad had the idea that if he created a bullet containing human bones, he would be able to take that fucking goat down without ever needing to get close.

BK: So, he wanted to kill you or your mom and have a nice supply of human bones?

Ian: That would be correct, but he told me that he loved us and that he couldn't go through with killing one of us. It sure didn't stop him trying to reach that point, though. From out of nowhere, the torture stopped. He came bursting through the front door one night after work, hugged my mom and tousled my hair, all with this big shit-eating grin on his face. He wolfed down his dinner that night and told me to come downstairs with him once I was done. He was positively bouncing off the fucking walls as he pulled a piece of bundled cloth out from his inside jacket pocket. He handled that thing like it was the most fragile thing ever, unwrapping it to reveal a decent sized chunk of bone.

I could tell by his behavior that this was not your average animal bone, yet I had no idea how he would have been able to get his hands on something human. It turns out that the fucking stuttering boy had found it wedged in the engine of the car that fucked up that girl in town. He finally had his human bone, and he wanted me to help prepare the bullets. We ground that bone down into powder and mixed it in with the gunpowder, although the truth of the matter is that there was more bone powder than anything in there. It took us a few days to make those bullets, during which I begged him to take me on the hunt. I saw this as my opportunity to get him out in the woods and into a situation where I could fucking kill him and sell it as a hunting accident. He would not let me come, though, saying that the hunt for the fucking goat was dangerous and that it was a job for men.

BK: Did he go out there on his own?

Ian: No. He had a regular hunting buddy called Pete Miller, a dude you are probably going to hear more about from someone else. Pete and my dad went out hunting a few days after the bullets were made, which was the last time we ever saw him alive.

BK: How did you find out that he had died?

Ian: They were gone a few days before people really started getting worried. There was talk about a search party being put together, but Pete came stumbling out of the woods before it was required. He was a fucking mess and looked like he had just stepped out of a war zone. His eyes were all glazed the fuck over, and he was mumbling incoherently. The town doctor gave him a shot of some sedative or another, after which he calmed down enough to tell what happened while they were gone.

He said that everything was fine at the start, but he said that my dad started acting a little nuts on the second day, talking about hunting a giant mystical fucking goat. Pete believed that the old man had snapped and suggested that they turn back, but dad ignored him. Pete was scared to leave him on his own, so he stuck with it, getting deeper and deeper into the woods with each forward step.

Pete was beginning to panic, but just as he was about to take one more shot at getting my dad to head back, he said that the old man started crying and pointing off in the distance. He kept repeating, "Do you see him, Pete, do you see him?" Pete said he couldn't see shit but trees and more trees, but the old man had his fucking weapon shouldered and was aiming at something off in the distance. The gun apparently jammed on the first shot, and when dad tried again, the whole thing just blew up in his face.

BK: The gun?

Ian: Yes, the fucking gun. Pete said that a big piece of shrapnel blew off and went right through my dad's eye, blowing off the back of his fucking skull. He also said that the whole area around my dad became covered in some sort of dust. The cops said it was probably smoke, but Pete insisted that it was dust and that it got in his eyes and nostrils, blinding him and making it hard to breathe for a couple of hours. I'm guessing it was the bone powder, but Pete could just as easily have been imagining things, although that seems a little less likely when you hear what happened to him after that. What happened to my dad after the accident was nothing short of fucking brutal. By the time they found him, most of his face had been eaten away, his eyes sucked out, and his brain totally gone. His stomach was torn open and his insides gutted. The bears and wolves in this region had themselves a fucking picnic over the course of a few days.

BK: Ugh! Can you tell me more about the aftermath, particularly in regard to Pete Miller?

Ian: That's not my story to tell, but I'm sure you'll hear all about it soon enough. They're about to play my song, so I have to get back. I'd love to say it was a pleasure meeting you, but it really fucking wasn't, so go fuck yourself.

Coal Miner's Daughter by Susan

BK: Hi there. Please have a seat. Are you okay with me recording our conversation?

Susan: Yes, sir, that would be fine.

BK: Oh, no need for formalities here. Please, call me Brian. And your name is?

Susan: Susan. Susan Miller.

BK: I just spoke to Ian, and he made mention of a Pete Miller in his story. Are you and Pete related?

Susan: Pete was my father. He is no longer with us, sir, but I still have some wonderful memories of him.

BK: You say "was your father." From that, I assume that he has passed on?

Susan: Yes, sir.

BK: Please accept my condolences, and, please, call me Brian.

Susan: My father was very big on women being respectful to men, so if it's okay with you, I would just as soon call you sir. Brian seems a little too familiar, especially since I am talking to a man I have just met.

BK: Okay, Susan, whatever makes you most comfortable. I really enjoyed your song choice. I am being presumptuous again, but am I correct in assuming that your father was a coal miner?

Susan: Yes, sir, he was.

BK: I know that a lot of people get sick after years down the mines. Is that what got your father?

Susan: No, sir. He certainly had fellow workers who had issues with black lung and other illnesses brought on by years down the mine. That was not the case with my father, though. He was always careful with his health, especially after we lost my mother to cancer. He would go for a complete physical twice per year, and he promised me that if they ever found anything, he would quit and do all he could to get better. He was very protective of me, to the point where he was not very keen on me leaving the house for reasons other than school.

BK: Were you okay with that? It doesn't seem like much of a life for a young girl.

Susan: It was all I ever really knew, sir. Even before my mother died, I was very rarely out of the house. My father worked hard to provide us with everything we needed, so my mother and I made sure that the house was always neat and tidy and that my father had clean clothes and a hot meal every night. I know other girls who hated doing housework, but I was fine with it. My mother always seemed very happy and grateful for all that she had and all that my father did for us, so why should I be unhappy with my lot?

BK: That's a very positive outlook that you have on life, Susan. How did things change after your mother passed away?

Susan: When she was ill, some of the other housewives in the town would come to help keep the house in order. My mother did the best she could while she was physically able, which was longer than most expected given that she didn't seek any type of treatment for her illness.

BK: Why not?

Susan: Well, sir, by the time she was diagnosed, the cancer had spread through quite a large portion of her body. The local doctor told her that there were treatments available, chemotherapy and such, but he also said that her prognosis was not particularly good. She didn't see the point in going back and forth to the nearest hospital where she could get the chemo she needed. It was a couple of hours round trip, which she viewed as nothing but wasted time.

BK: Did your father not try to talk her into getting treatment?

Susan: No, sir. He was very much a traditionalist in a lot of ways. He believed that a woman's place was in the home, but he also never demanded that my mother simply submit to his beliefs. She actually had a part-time job at a diner in the next town over for a little while, a job she took with my father's blessing. She didn't really care for it, though, and only lasted a couple of months before she quit to be back home full-time. She always told me that our home was where she felt most comfortable and that looking after me and my father was the most fulfilling job she could ever hope to have. I took that to heart and basically assumed her housekeeping role after she passed. I was still too young to do it all on my own though, but the neighbors helped until it was clear that I could handle it all.

BK: How did your father feel about that?

Susan: He never really said anything one way or the other, sir, although he did tell me that I needed to finish high school. I was all for dropping out and staying home, but he told me that he wouldn't be around forever and that I needed to have an education so that I could have what he called a positive future.

BK: What do you do now?

Susan: The same as I did back then, I look after the home. When my father died, I found out that he had taken out a life insurance policy many years prior. I had nothing left to pay on the house, as it was one of the original homes in Redfield and had long since been paid off by previous generations of my family. It probably explains why the stuff that we had growing up was just a little better than what my friends had. We frequently decorated and updated our furniture, and I never remember us having a car for more than a few years at a time. We certainly weren't well off, but compared to a lot of folks in town, we lived quite comfortably. I have more than enough money to maintain the house and do what I want.

BK: Don't you want to go to college or have some sort of career?

Susan: I don't see the reason for either, sir. I learned all I need to know in high school, and I have plenty to keep me busy during the course of any given day. There are my daily chores to attend to, after which I read a little or sometimes write in my journal. I do enjoy writing.

BK: Have you ever considered starting a blog? That's what I do. You can make a nice little bit of money if you can build up a good following.

Susan: I don't know what a blog is or how I would start one, sir.

BK: Oh, it's really very easy. It's just like writing in your journal, save for the fact that you do it all online and share your thoughts with the world.

Susan: That's definitely not for me. I don't even have one of those fancy phones, never mind a computer, and I really have no interest in sharing what I write with anyone. I enjoy sitting down and putting my thoughts on paper. It's like having a conversation with a good friend, one who will never let you down.

BK: Don't you have any friends that you can talk to about your day?

Susan: I have plenty of people that I know and that I say hello to when I go into town for groceries, but I'm sure they have better things to do than stand around talking to me. I am always very civil, sir, but I really have nothing too interesting to tell.

BK: Yet, here you are talking to me, Susan, and I must say that I am very interested to hear what you have to tell me about being the coal miner's daughter that you sing about. That song must mean something to you for you to sing it so often. Did you know that there was a movie of the same name, all about the life of Loretta Lynn?

Susan: No, sir, I don't know anything about that movie. I have a TV at home, but I rarely have it switched on, and I certainly don't spend any time at the movie theater in town. Those movies all seem to be very long, and it all just seems like a waste of time. I'm a lot like my mother in how I value my time. As for the song, it may seem as though I sing it to pay homage to my father, but the truth is that I don't really know why I do. I'm happy at home, but there is something inside me that tells me to come here and sing, and it's always that song.

BK: There's no other song that comes to mind that you would like to try?

Susan: No, sir.

BK: Well then, do you mind if we just go back and talk a little more about your father and your life leading up to his passing?

Susan: No, sir, I don't mind at all. Where would you like me to begin?

BK: Let's go back to the time after your mother died. How did your father react after she died?

Susan: My father was very stoic. He wasn't an unhappy man by any stretch of the imagination, but he also wasn't overly serious. It's just that he was very guarded when it came to his emotions. He was always very kind to my mother and me and would frequently bring home little gifts for us on payday. He made sure to be extra kind to me in the weeks and months following my mother's passing, and he would frequently ask how I was feeling and if I wanted to talk. I would oftentimes cry and tell him that I missed mother so much, and he would hold me in his arms and give me all the comfort I needed. I never did see him shed a tear, though, but there were a couple of times when I could hear him crying out in the living room. I so wanted to go out there and comfort him the same way he did me, but I was afraid that seeing him cry would somehow change how I felt about him. I can't explain why I felt that way, sir, so please don't ask.

BK: Of course not, Susan. Did your father not date other woman in the years after your mother's death?

Susan: No, sir. There were a lot of women in and out of the house after my mother passed, but they were all there to help, nothing more. There was one lady who obviously had a thing for him, but he wasn't interested. He would always be kind and respectful to that woman, but he also made it clear that his romantic days were over. I once heard him telling her that my mother and I were the only women he had ever loved and that in terms of love and affection, she could never be replaced. She, her name escapes me, started coming around less and less often, and the last I heard, she had moved out of town with another man.

BK: What about you? You're an attractive woman, if you don't mind me saying. Did you ever go out on any dates?

Susan: My father made it quite clear that gentlemen callers would not be abided until I had turned 18 years of age. Yes, sir, there were a few boys who asked me out on a date, but I always turned them down as politely as I could. Craig Black was the most persistent of the lot, and while I did find him to be rather cute, I was also a little scared of him. I can't really say what it was about him that put the fear in me, but it turns out that my thoughts about him were correct. He was indeed a bad apple.

Craig made the mistake of coming to my house one night, apparently doing so with the idea of asking my father for permission to date me. It was the only time in my life that I ever saw my father show anger, and I really thought for a moment that he was going to hit Craig. Once he had shooed him away, my father warned me about Craig and said that I should steer well clear of him. I let father know that I had already turned down his advances several times and that I had done nothing to give the idea that I might be in any way interested in dating. That seemed to cool my father down considerably, and it was the only conversation we ever had on the subject of Craig Black.

BK: Thank you, Susan. I think I now have a rather solid idea of what your life was like with both your parents alive, as well as when you lived alone with your father. I'd like to now talk about his passing. Was it sudden?

Susan: That really depends on how you look at it, sir. My father was always an incredibly healthy man, probably because he never smoked and he didn't drink much. My mother always made healthy, home-cooked meals, and while he probably had a few sick days, I can honestly say that I don't remember him ever missing work. He was as healthy as it gets until the day he returned home from that hunting trip with Mr. Miller. He went downhill very quickly after that, turning into a shadow of the man that I grew up with. So, yes, in that regard, his passing was a little sudden.

BK: Tell me what you remember about that hunting trip and the events that came after.

Susan: My father was an avid hunter, and he would regularly head out into the woods with Mr. Bryce. He would usually only be gone a day or two at most; I think because he was concerned about what might happen to me when he was away. I'm sure he felt some guilt at not doing more to get my mother to seek treatment, but he really shouldn't have. The end result would have been the same even if she had gone for chemotherapy. I was never worried about him when he was away hunting. He had never gotten into any kind of trouble, and he always returned when he said he would. I was scared when he left that time, though. I had a big knot in my belly the entire time.

BK: Why was that?

Susan: Well, sir, it wasn't anything that my father was doing that caused me concern. It was the way in which Mr. Bryce was behaving that was the most troublesome. I always found him to be a nice, kind man, but he was short with me the day he came to pick up my father for that hunt, plus he just seemed, I don't know how to put it, frantic, I guess. He was pacing back and forth and kept yelling at my father to hurry up and get ready. He kept talking about a big score out in the woods and how he needed to get to it before anyone else did. My father laughed the whole thing off and told him to be patient, but I could see in my father's eyes that he was a little worried about how Mr. Bryce was acting.

BK: Did he say anything about it to you before he left?

Susan: No, sir. He told me to look after the house and that he would be back within forty-eight hours. Everything was normal with my father, but that crazed look that Mr. Bryce had on his face set me right on edge.

BK: How long did they end up being gone and when did you really start to worry?

Susan: As soon as the two-day mark passed, my level of concern started to spike. My father was never late, sir, never, and the fact that he was getting later by the minute told me that something had gone seriously wrong out there. I called the town sheriff and told him how worried I was, but he just laughed at me and told me that my father could look after himself and that everything would be fine. I wanted to believe him, but there was something eating away at my insides. I believed that worry was going to swallow me whole, the way the cancer did with my mother. By the time we got to day four, the sheriff listened and promised to get some men out there. It was the sixth day away from home that they eventually found my father, although he had almost made it back on his own by that point. He was tired and weak, so they took him right to the hospital in the next town over. The sheriff was nice enough to come and get me and take me to my father's bedside.

BK: How did he look?

Susan: Hollow, sir. He looked as though all the life had been drained out of him while he was away. He had a faraway look in his eyes for a couple of days, to the point where I'm not so sure that he even saw me sitting beside him. I spent the whole time talking to him and telling him how much I loved him, and while he may not have seen me, I know he heard me. His eyes would flick a little in my direction when I was talking, and he would give my hand a little squeeze every now and again, but I don't remember him once looking me in the eye for those two days. He was seeing someone, though, because I could see his eyes moving as though he was tracking movements within the room. It scared me a little, but I forgot about it once he snapped out of it and said that he was ready to come home and get back to work. The doctors cleared him quite quickly, although they did make him take a week off work. It drove my father nuts, but he did as he was told.

BK: How was he when he got back home?

Susan: On the surface, he seemed to be doing okay, but there were times when I would see him get that faraway look in his eyes again. It usually happened when he thought I wasn't paying any attention, as though he was trying to hide the fact that he was somewhere else other than in his own home. Things got much worse when he went back down the mine.

BK: What happened then?

Susan: He stopped eating and was having difficulty sleeping. When he did nod off, he would wake up screaming, always yelling at someone to leave him alone. I was terrified, and I asked him what was going on, what he was seeing. He wouldn't tell me at first, but then after one particularly rough nightmare, he told me everything. He said that he had breathed in some of the dust that came out of Mr. Bryce's gun and that it was driving him crazy. He kept seeing a strange man everywhere he went, even claiming that the man's face was carved into the wall in the area of the mine where he worked. Hitting it did no good, he said, as chipping away the rock just seemed to make the face look that much clearer.

BK: My God. What about at home?

Susan: Yes, sir, he saw him there, too, both asleep and while he was awake. My father said that things were worse when he slept because the stranger would come and whisper awful things in his ear. He started to miss work after that and barely had the strength to stand. They eventually came and took him back to the hospital, but nothing they did helped. He would tear out the IV's that were pumping fluids and sedatives into his body, all the while yelling that they had to get that man out of his room. They eventually took to strapping him down to the bed to stop him doing any damage to himself. Once they did that, he slept a lot, but he always woke up in a fit of outright terror. I never left his side the whole time that he was there and it was on the day he passed that he told me to lean in close, that he needed to tell me something.

BK: What did he say?

Susan: He asked me to look in the corner of the room and describe the man that I saw standing there. I looked and looked, wanting to believe that my father was seeing something real, but no-one was there. I told him that I needed a little bit of help and that maybe he should describe what the man looked like. That's what he did, going into every little detail about the stranger's features, down to the number of wrinkles around his eyes and the length of his fingernails, which he said were longer on the right hand. I saw nothing, but I am sure my father did, such was the detail of his description. I have…

BK: How soon did he pass after that conversation?

Susan: It was a matter of minutes, sir. I was truly shaken by what he had said, so I waited until he nodded off, at which point I went to get myself a cup of coffee. The coffee room was at the end of the hall where my father was situated in the hospital. I was just enjoying my first sip when an alarm started going off, and people started yelling about a code blue. I had no idea what was happening, but when I heard them yell my father's room number, I went rushing back down the hall to be with him. They wouldn't let me in, but I could see them working on him. Everything was total madness for a few minutes, and then it all just stopped. When the doctor in charge of my father saw me, he came out and took me aside, letting me know that despite their best efforts, my father had passed. It was only later on that I found out that he had used his teeth to sever his tongue, which he then swallowed, choking himself to death. I'm told that he kept his lips clamped shut and wouldn't budge until he finally stopped breathing. Even then, they said that they had to force his mouth open.

BK: I am so sorry, Susan, that must have been awful for you.

Susan: It was, sir, but things are a whole lot worse now.

BK: What? How so?

Susan: I tried to tell you, sir, just a moment ago, but you interrupted me. The thing is, the man that my father described, he's here now.

BK: Where?

Susan: Don't look, sir. He'll know I'm talking about him. He keeps watching you, so I'm sure he will come and chat soon enough. I've said enough, and now I just want to go home.

One Bourbon, One Scotch, One Beer by Harold

Harold: What's up? How you holding up, my man?

BK: I'm fine, I think, although I appear to be getting a whole lot more than I bargained for when I first sat down. I've been trying to make sense of all the stories that I've been hearing, but nothing seems to be adding up. I'm a little disoriented if I'm being honest.

Harold: Relax, chief. Just sit back and enjoy the yarns. I'm sure it'll all make sense once we all get to have our say. I'm Harold, by the way, but go ahead and call me Harry. I've never been much of a fan of my full name.

BK: Okay, Harry. Why don't you like the name? It's a rather dignified moniker if you ask me.

Harold: Nah, it makes me sound like an old fart, which probably isn't surprising given that I'm named after some distant relative. It turns out my family was one of the first to put down roots here in Redfield, so I guess I'm supposed to feel honored at being named for a town legend. My last name has given me a little more pull in this neck of the woods than my first, so Harry it is, chief.

BK: Harry it shall be then. Why don't we start out by talking about the song that you were singing? Do you like classic rock or are you just a fan of booze?

Harold: Both, although neither are my reason for belting that tune out. Given the story that I have to tell, it's probably not the greatest song selection to make, yet it's the one that always seems to call my name, despite the awful memories it conjures up.

BK: Are you okay with jumping right into the awful parts or would you rather ease into things a little more gently?

Harold: Let's just chill a little before I rehash the awfulness, chief. Look, I saw how long you spent with the rest of the weirdos in this place, so I'd like a little slice of that chatting action if you don't mind. Besides, we really don't get very many visitors here, so it'd be nice to talk to someone other than the voices in my head.

BK: You hear voices in your head?

Harold: Just a figure of speech, chief. I mean, don't we all have that little inner voice that chirps away day and night?

BK: Yes, I suppose we do, Harry. I spend a lot of time alone with my thoughts, but I suppose I've never really thought of it as voices in my head.

Harold: Maybe because yours is the only voice that you hear, chief. I hear all sorts up there, but don't worry, they don't tell me to do anything bad unless you think my singing voice is a little rough on the old ears. Ha-ha.

BK: You sounded just fine to me.

Harold: Ass kisser. You don't need to blow smoke up my poop trumpet to get my story. I'm going to tell it to you whether you want to hear it or not.

BK: I'm not...

Harold: I kid, I kid. Relax, chief; I'm just trying to have a little fun. I was always known as the class clown, and that has never gone away. I'm a chain yanker. Always have been, always will be. You're going to be begging for the lighthearted version of me once we get down to the nitty gritty here, but like I said, let's just take a moment to chillax and get to know each other a little. You still haven't told me your name.

BK: Oh, my apologies. It's Brian, Brian Keane. I'm a writer here to do a piece about dive bars in Georgia. This joint wasn't on my list, but I stumbled upon it by accident.

Harold: I'm not a big believer in accidents or coincidences, chief. We usually end up where we are for a reason, even if our internal GPS got all scrambled and took us somewhere unexpected. You should see your face, chief. Here I am talking about voices and sat-nav's in my head and you just sitting there looking at me as though you just became a guest at the Mad Hatter's tea party. I'm no more messed up than the average dude; I'm just not worried about appearances, which is why I say what's on my mind and in the way I'm most comfortable saying it. You get me, chief?

BK: It's not you, Harry, honestly. I'm feeling just a little out of sorts is all.

Harold: I get that. This place will do it to you, which is probably why visitors are so damned scarce. Why don't we just move on so you can get back to asking your questions? How does that sound, chief?

BK: That would be good. Where is the best place for you to start your story?

Harold: Redfield High School is probably the best jumping off point, chief. That will give me a chance to introduce you to the other folks in my story. There were four of us involved, all told, but only one of us made it out. Since we are sitting here talking, it stands to reason that I am the sole survivor, right? Or maybe it was someone else, and you are talking to a ghost. BOO!!

BK: Jesus!!

Harold: Ha-ha. You are one easy to spook bunny, chief. You have got to relax, or you are never going to get through your time here in one piece.

BK: Maybe I should have a drink.

Harold: Good luck with that, chief. The service here is non-existent, and I think the booze bottles are all actually bone dry. You could get yourself a co-cola, but if you are looking to lace that bad boy with some liquid courage, you are going to need to get up and get back on the road that leads to liquor town. There used to be a dude in Redfield that made moonshine, but that all came to an end a while back when his pecker got in the way of business. Now, that one's a good story, but not mine to tell. Bet you're hearing that line a lot.

BK: I am. I guess I'll just have to be patient and let everyone have their turn.

Harold: Now you're getting it, chief. Sit back and go with the flow and you'll end up feeling a whole lot more relaxed. I can't say that you won't still feel a little upside down and inside out, but good things come to those that wait. Isn't that what they say?

BK: Indeed. Okay, Harry, I'll take your advice. Let's get back to your high school years, shall we?

Harold: Ha-ha. Thought you'd never ask. Now, I believe I said that our glorious home to education was called Redfield High School, but in fact, its full name was Redfield Harold Haskins Memorial High School, named after the same family member whose name I now carry around. Can you imagine how cuckoo it was to go to a high school that bore your name? I figured I'd be in for a bit of a ribbing because of it, so I took action to make sure that I got ahead of all that nonsense. On the first day of my first high school year, I showed up in a homemade crown and cape and demanded that everyone refer to me as King Harold of Redfield High. It was a move that could have backfired, but everyone got a kick out of it, even the seniors, so I was essentially left alone right from the start. The problem was that I was expected to keep the fun coming, which was why I slipped right into the role of the class clown.

BK: Maybe even the King of the class clowns, huh, Harry?

Harold: Ha-ha. Now you're getting into the spirit, chief. I like that. Anyway, that move made me a bit of a minor celebrity in school, but given that I was a member of the Redfield Haskins clan, one of the founding families, I was also expected to be among the brightest and best. Yeah, I spent a lot of time mucking about in school and being a bit of a pain in the ass, but I also worked hard and got good grades. As long as I did that, the teachers, and more importantly, my parents left me alone and let me have my fun. I never did anything malicious or hurtful, so it really was all seen as being a bit of harmless hijinks. I ended up being the most popular kid in school by the time senior year rolled around, but I hung out with a very small group of friends.

BK: Who were those kids?

Harold: Craig Black was my best friend all through high school. You'll have heard some terrible things about him already, and you are going to hear more in a few minutes, but when I first met him, he was a great kid. He was quiet, but he had a dark sense of humor that cracked me up. Best of all, he was more than willing to help me plan my pranks, playing straight man to my class clown. I know that after he went to work at the scrapyard, he used some of my best pranks on one of the guys that worked there, the dude that ended up with the stutter. I saw him change through high school, though, and I was starting to distance myself from him a little towards the end, but I never did get the chance to break free the way I wanted to.

The other two in my group were both girls. There was Mel, who was my girlfriend. She wasn't any kind of beauty or anything, chief, but she was sweet and smart and a whole lot better looking than most of the other girls in Redfield, which didn't take much, to be honest. The other girl was Kelly, who was Mel's best friend. She was a little annoying, mostly because she spent most of her time in my presence asking whether Craig was interested in her, which he wasn't. Yes, he slept with her a few times in our senior year, but it was more about busting a nut than having any kind of feelings for her. He was starting to slip off the deep end a little by that point, so no real surprise that he used Kelly that way.

BK: I hear he was interested in other girls in town.

Harold: That's true enough, chief, but he always went after the ones who were the most unattainable. He had a rather unhealthy obsession with Susan, who you've met already, which almost ended with him getting a beating from her dad. The girl was pretty cute, but she was damn near a shut-in and had some serious daddy issues. He eventually took the hint when Susan's dad got involved, but then he turned his eye to Ursula. I'm not sure what he was thinking since we all knew she was gay, but that didn't stop him. I wasn't there the night she went off on him, but I heard all about it on the night when he finally snapped.

BK: Wait, I'm confused. How did he end up in a bar fight with Ursula when he wasn't old enough to be there? Twenty-one is the drinking age in Georgia, and you are talking about events happening right after high school.

Harold: That's true, chief, but the bar most kids went to didn't give a shit about your age. As long as you kept your nose clean and didn't cause a fuss, the bar owners and the cops turned a blind eye. There was always trouble at that bar, but it was usually started by the miners who came in after a long shift. Craig did lose his underage drinking privileges that night with Ursula, though, which is why we ended up where we did.

BK: And where was that?

Harold: There's an abandoned campground just outside of town that sits on a lake that is mostly nothing but a cesspool now. It's not the most glamorous spot in the world, but there are fire pits there, as well as some huts that you can hunker down in if the weather takes a turn for the worse. It's a popular drinking spot on the weekends, but it's generally dead during the week. Anyway, after the incident at the bar, Craig calls and suggests that we get together for a drink or six. He sounded pretty buzzed when he called, so while I agreed to meet up the next night, I was certain that he would forget all about it once he sobered up. That proved not to be the case. He called again the next morning, telling me to bring Mel and Kelly along so that we could make a night of it. Craig said that he would take care of the beer and that I should pick up a bottle of liquor. I had just woken up when he called, so I couldn't think of a valid excuse that would get me out of it. Long story short, I called the girls and told them to get ready for a little night out.

BK: How did they react to that?

Harold: Mel was always really easygoing and would essentially just roll along with whatever plan I came up with. Kelly was an even easier sell, as she was always game to spend some time with Craig. I hadn't seen Craig in about a month, so I was actually pretty psyched to meet up and have a few brews. Sure, it was still in my head that he had been acting weird for a while, but with that time apart, it was easy to convince myself that I was probably imagining that things were worse than they really were.

BK: But you were wrong about that?

Harold: I was way wrong, chief, way wrong. Things started out normal enough, to the point where it felt as though we had rolled back time a little. We spoke about all the dumb shit that we did in high school, and Craig kept bowing and calling me His Highness when I would talk about the pranks I pulled. We were all having a good time, but while me and the girls seemed to mellow out with each passing drink, Craig started to laugh less and become a little more subdued the more he drank.

The conversation started to hit a lull, and it became clear to me that we had little in common anymore. All we had to talk about was the past, which was cool and all, but you could feel things start to get a little awkward and forced. Kelly was oblivious, though, and she kept getting friendlier and friendlier with Craig, making it obvious that she was game for a little outdoor fun. He wasn't that interested in her at the start of the night, but he eventually caved, and they took off for one of the old huts.

BK: What did you and Mel do then?

Harold: We both started talking about calling it a night and heading home, but I said we should probably wait until the other two got back. I wasn't sure how Craig got to the campground, so I wanted to make sure we could give Kelly a ride home. I told Mel I would drive, so she lifted the last beer out of the cooler and had one for the road. We didn't have to wait very long. Craig and Kelly came back about 15 minutes or so after they had left for their romantic interlude. It was obvious that something was wrong.

BK: How so?

Harold: Craig looked pissed, man, I mean seriously angry. He had his fists clenched and was repeatedly punching himself in the leg. Kelly was trailing just a little way behind him and looked as white as a ghost. BOO! Okay, not funny this time. Anyway, Craig sits down by the fire pit, and I can hear him mumbling some incoherent shit. I say incoherent, but you could hear little bits of what he was saying, little nuggets about stuck-up bitches and fucked-up dudes. It was more than a little scary and Mel was digging her nails into my leg as he rambled on. It hurt like hell, but it gave me the clarity I needed to try and cool the tension that was building.

I put my hand on Craig's shoulder and asked him what was wrong. He shrugged my hand off and told me not to touch him and that he hadn't given me permission. He said it was people like me that made it impossible for him to get it up, whatever the hell that meant, chief. Kelly then tried to calm him down, telling him that everything was okay and that it was all her fault, at which time I put two and two together and realized that he was having some performance issues. He had drunk a lot that night, so it really wasn't a total shocker. I mean, we've all be there, right, chief?

BK: Yes, of course.

Harold: Anyway, when Kelly said that, he wheeled on her and drew back like he was going to slug her. He never did, but he held his clenched fist up in the air for what seemed like an eternity before fishing in the cooler for a beer. It all turned to shit when that fishing trip came up empty. He picked up the cooler and tossed it into the woods, screaming in a total fit of rage and demanding to know who had taken his last beer. I was about to say that I had taken it when Mel piped up and admitted to drinking it. She was as cool as a cucumber, which struck me as odd given that I was close to shitting my pants. She told him that she was sorry and that we would take him into town and buy him a six-pack on the way home.

BK: How did he react to that?

Harold: For a moment, I thought that Mel's voice of reason had done the trick because he went quiet and just stared at her. He seemed to relax for a moment, but then he just lost it. He was pointing at Mel and screaming that he was going to kill her, at which point Kelly jumped up and threw herself at him, hugging him and trying to calm him down. He shrugged her off as though she weighed nothing, and as she stumbled away from him, she fell back into the fire pit. Her hair went up like a Roman candle, but she just laid there and let it happen. To be fair, it took Mel and me a moment to react, but Craig beat us to it. Just as we were about to haul Kelly out of there, he stepped forward and put his foot on her chest, holding her down in the flames. I could see her try to scream then, but there was no sound coming from her save for some cracking and popping as her skin blistered and broke. Craig just stood there grinning at us, looking like the cat that got the cream, and he didn't seem to notice that his boot was melting, and the bottom of his jeans were starting to catch fire. When he did, he let out a little yelp and took his foot off Kelly's chest. I saw that as our chance to get the fuck out of Dodge, so I pulled on Mel and told her to run.

BK: What did Craig do then?

Harold: He very calmly informed us that we weren't going anywhere because he wasn't done with us yet. I chose to disagree, and I bolted, reaching for Mel as I went. She turned to follow but tripped and went down hard. The damsel in distress tripping and falling is perhaps the most clichéd scene in every horror movie, but now I know that shit is real. He was on her in a second, dragging her up by her hair. Mel had no fight in her, and it looked as though she had hit her head on the way down. Her eyes were all glassy, and there was blood streaming down the right side of her face.

Craig was smiling again, but he still looked far from happy, chief. He asked me where I was going and demanded to know why I allowed my woman to drink that last beer. By this point, I was screaming at him to let her go and promising that I would kill him if he hurt her. He seemed to take that as a dare because he pulled a shitty pocket knife out of his pants and jammed it into the side of her neck. My legs almost went out from under me, but I got myself together and took a run at him. He tossed Mel aside, that knife still wedged in there, and took a swing at me when I got close. I'm guessing the booze slowed him down because he never came close to making contact. I heard the air rush out of him as I tackled him to the ground. The impact seemed to take all the fight out of him, and he just looked at me with tears in his eyes, the sight of which took some of the fight out of me.

BK: Why was that?

Harold: He looked just like a little kid. Totally scared and totally alone. It was the smell of burning flesh and Mel's moaning for help that snapped me out of it. I hit him hard a few times and then crawled over to Mel to try and help her. One look at Kelly and you could tell that there was nothing to be done. There was no phone service out in the woods, so I decided to carry Mel out and get her to the hospital.

That was when Craig hit me from behind and started raving about killing us again. He took me by surprise because I thought I had put him out cold, so he quickly got the upper hand, straddling me and choking the life out of me. I remember weird black spots before my eyes and thinking that I was going to die when the pressure suddenly stopped. I'd had my eyes closed to try and block out those spots, and when I opened them, I saw Craig falling off me with the knife sticking out of his eye.

BK: Mel?

Harold: That's right, chief, my Mel. She pulled that knife right out her neck and jabbed that fucker to save my life. She had her hand over the neck wound, but blood was spraying everywhere. All I could do was hold her and watch as she slipped away. It was only when I was losing her that I realized that she was the queen in my kingdom. I told her I loved her, over and over again, but I don't know if she heard me. I like to think that she did because when the light went out of her eyes, she had the sweetest little smile on her face. I hated Craig, but I ended up feeling sympathetic towards him once I got to hear his story.

BK: What was that?

Harold: Oh, come on, chief. Surely you must know the rules by now. One person, one story. I've told mine, so now it's time for someone else to take a turn.

Piece by Piece by Marie

BK: What was all that about? Are you okay?

Marie: What are you talking about?

BK: Well, it looked and sounded as though you were about to sing something different before that man started whispering in your ear. What did he say to you?

Marie: That's the boss.

BK: Does he own this place?

Marie: I don't know about that, but I do know that he's in charge of the music. He calls the shots, and he felt that it would be better if I sung "Piece by Piece" instead of my usual.

BK: Why would he care?

Marie: Among other things, he told me that we should be making every effort to put on a big show for our esteemed guest, which I suppose is you.

BK: I'm not sure what he's talking about. Sorry, I didn't get your name, mine's Brian.

Marie: Marie. I don't know what to tell you about that. All I know is what he tells me, and it's always better to just play along and do what he asks.

BK: Does he hurt you? I can...

Marie: You can't do anything, and I'm not here to talk about any of that. I'm just here to tell you my story. That's why you are here, isn't it? You want stories. Answers that will make our little world seem a little clearer. I can get you a little closer to those answers, but you need to stop worrying about the smaller things and simply listen to the stories being told.

BK: This certainly seems to be a strange town. How can so many bad things have happened in a place this far off the beaten path?

Marie: Again, you are asking questions that I don't have answers for. Why don't I just get to my story, and why don't you just focus on the task at hand?

BK: Okay then. Answer me this; what was the song that you were originally going to sing before the boss told you to change it?

Marie: Now, that's a question I can answer. It was "The Thunder Rolls."

BK: The Garth Brooks song?

Marie: Uh-huh.

BK: Can we talk about that one first before we get to the Kelly Clarkson tune?

Marie: They are both part of the same story, but it is probably best if we go back to the beginning and talk about my life growing up here. Doing that will present you with the full picture, which I'm sure is what you are after. Plus, the boss wants you to be entertained, so why paint a smaller picture when the bigger one has more delightful details?

BK: Start wherever you like, Marie. I have nothing but time.

Marie: Hmm, not true, but okay.

BK: What do you…

Marie: I was born in Redfield and other than a few trips in-state, I have never really left for any great length of time. My family helped grow and work the strawberry fields in the early days, with future generations of my clan deciding that it was a good idea to stay and keep things the way they have always been. Change was something to be feared, so my parent took the path most traveled.

BK: Why did you stay?

Marie: For my mom. She was more than just my mom; she was also my best friend. I knew it would break her heart if I moved away, plus I couldn't stand the idea of her being stuck here alone with HIM!!

BK: Your father?

Marie: No, he passed away when I was little. I don't remember a lot about him, but the memories that I do have are all good. My mom would often talk about their life together and what a wonderful man he was. My dad was absolutely the love of her life, but the cigarettes took him early. Mom was still very young and eventually began craving some companionship again. She wasn't looking for anything serious, but that's usually when serious finds you.

BK: She started dating?

Marie: Yes. She waited more than three years to get back out there after losing my dad, which should give you some idea of how heartbroken she was. My mom was a beautiful woman and always had men paying her attention. Finding dates wasn't difficult for her, but she would go on one or two with each man before ending it and moving on to the next. I don't necessarily think she was being picky, but rather just holding her dates to a ridiculously high standard. She was looking for someone just like my dad, which was something she was never ever going to find.

BK: But she did eventually find someone?

Marie: Oh, I'd say he found her. My mom was an English teacher at Haskins and would routinely meet with parents to update them on how their kids were doing. She was a firm believer in having parents play a role in their child's education, so she went above and beyond to make sure that they were studying at home as well as when they were in her classroom. There were a few people that came to those meetings as a couple despite being divorced or in the process of getting there. One of the men in that group took a real shine to my mom and actively started chasing her.

BK: How did he do that?

Marie: He would contact the school and ask if he could talk to my mom about his son's progress in English class. He would always paint it as being concerned for the future of his son and the college he would eventually go to. My mom was impressed that a parent would take the time to play such an active role and always made time for him. It became clear quite quickly that she was smitten with him.

BK: How so?

Marie: In the beginning, she would talk about him in a strictly professional tone, but once she found out that he was single and on the market, things started to change. She took to getting out of bed a little earlier on the days she was to meet with him, fussing over what to wear and taking real care in applying her make-up, which she usually didn't wear very often. She still spoke to me about the meetings and how wonderful he was as a father, but she would also tell me how polite he was and how good he looked in his suit. It was nice to see her so happy, and I was initially glad that she had found someone that she liked.

BK: When did that feeling change for you?

Marie: Not until much later. When they officially started dating he, Martin Jackson was his name, would come to the house to pick my mom up. He was always right on time, and she was always fashionably late in getting ready for the date, so there was always some time for him and I to sit and talk. He was genuinely interested in what I had to say, asking about my schooling, my plans for the future, and a whole bunch of other stuff that only my mom ever seemed really interested in. He struck me as a really nice man, and I remember being glad that he had come into our lives. Before he proposed to my mom, he came and asked for my permission to do so. When I said yes, he also asked if I would help him pick out a ring that my mom would love. I was excited to be a part of something so grown-up, so of course, I agreed to help him find something special for my mom.

BK: How old were you then?

Marie: I was eleven. I was getting to an age where my tomboy ideals were becoming a thing of the past, and I think that was because of my mom. She would always dress up really nice and make herself look so pretty, and I wanted to look and behave just like her, which meant ditching the dungarees that I always wore. Martin said that as a reward for helping with the ring, he would take me on a shopping spree when we went to Atlanta to visit the jewelry stores, and that's exactly what he did. He took me back home with one small box containing the biggest diamond I had ever seen, while I walked in the front door carrying a mountain of bags filled with new dresses and shoes.

My mom knew that I was taking a trip to Atlanta with Martin, but she thought it was for something else entirely. I don't really know what he told her we were up to, but she certainly looked surprised, and a little angry, when I walked in carrying all that stuff. Her anger disappeared very quickly when Martin dropped down on one knee and proposed. It was probably the most perfect moment of my young life, and I remember all three of us hugging and crying after my mom said yes. I felt like the second luckiest girl in the world, with my mom sitting just ahead of me on that list.

BK: It all sounds wonderful, but I'm guessing it didn't stay that way?

Marie: It did for a while. Heck, I even took to calling him dad, although I did ask mom if it was okay for me to do so. She took a moment to answer when I asked, almost as though she were looking for permission from my real dad and waiting for a reply.

She said that it would be fine, but thinking about it after the fact, I'm sure there was a little bit of hurt in her eyes. It was a fleeting thing, and I might be imagining it all these years later, but I really do think it was there.

BK: Were she and Martin still in a good place when you made that request?

Marie: As far as I could tell, yes. They were always really lovey-dovey and happy, and I never heard them argue or sensed any tension. Things changed when he got a promotion at work. Martin was employed by a big auto parts supplier that had offices a couple of towns over from Redfield. Rather than uprooting us after the engagement, he decided to move into our home, which meant a little bit of a commute each day. It wasn't a long haul by any stretch of the imagination, and he said that he enjoyed the travel as it gave him time to decompress after a hard day at work.

He was offered a job as the regional sales manager for the company, and while he would still be based in his usual office, he was also expected to travel quite a bit. I remember him calling a family meeting and discussing it with mom and me. None of us fancied the idea of him being away, but mom felt that it would be unfair to hold him back from a career advancement and the money that came with it. Mom said he should take the job and we went out for a big celebration dinner that night. It was the last time I remember us all being happy together under the same roof.

BK: What went wrong?

Marie: The new job changed Martin, and not for the better. He was always a very confident man, which was part of the reason why he was so good at his job, but he eventually crossed the line between confidence and arrogance. The company he worked for was already big and successful, but his region became the best in the country under his leadership, or at least that was the way he told it. He stopped asking mom and me about our day, choosing instead to talk about his. He didn't head out of town much in the first couple of months on the job, but after that, I remember him being gone for long spells at a time. I'm talking two or three weeks per trip before coming home for a few days and heading back out.

When he was home, my mom practically begged for attention, but he was too busy either talking about work or disappearing into his home office to make those "important calls." When mom or I complained, he would get indignant and tell us that he was working hard to provide us with a better life. He told us that we couldn't understand what it was like to be the man of the house and to handle the responsibilities as such. I'm sure he was totally forgetting that my mom did all that in the years between my dad dying and meeting him. He basically turned into a real dick, but then he got even worse.

BK: Worse how?

Marie: He started to become abusive to my mom, although only verbally at first. He started small, complaining about her looks and her cooking. He told her that since he was working so hard, the least she could do was make an effort to look good for him when he came home. I always thought she was amazingly pretty, and I know she made an extra effort on the days he would get back from traveling, but it was never enough. Dinner times were the worst, though, as he would spit out her food and talk about how awful it was compared to the high-end restaurants that he ate at when on the road. The real turning point came the night that he decided to throw his plate across the dining room table, barely missing my mom's head. He jumped out of his chair and grabbed her, shoving her face against the wall and screaming at her to lick the mess clean.

BK: What did you do?

Marie: I lost my shit. I was about sixteen or seventeen when this went down, and I was going through a goth phase at the time, all black clothes, hair, and make-up, all of which I figured would turn me into a tough chick not to be messed with. It wasn't really an act of rebellion though, as I think I was going dark to make my mom appear brighter somehow. Anyway, I charged at Martin and tried to drag him off, but he swatted me away as though I was nothing.

BK: He hit you?

Marie: Not really, no. He just pushed out to keep me at arm's length, and it was really my momentum that sent me spilling backward so quickly. I hit the edge of the table, which hurt, and that made me even angrier than I already was. I picked up a breadknife off the table and yelled at him to leave my mom alone. His face transformed into something truly monstrous when he saw me holding that knife, and I could see the knuckles on his free hand turn white as he clenched his fist. You could see that he was furious, but his voice remained calm and authoritative when he spoke. He called me a spoiled little bitch and told me to drop the knife or he would really hurt my mom. I wasn't about to call his bluff, so I dropped it and took a step back. I think that my attacking him took some of the fire out of the situation because he let my mom go the moment I put the knife back where it belonged.

BK: What happened in the aftermath?

Marie: Martin bolted out the door in a hurry and stayed away all night. I told my mom that we needed to call the police and let them know what happened, but she rejected that idea out of hand. Instead, she started clearing the table as she always did right after every meal. There were still pieces of food stuck in her hair, and she had an ugly red mark on the side of her face that had been pressed against the wall. I tried to help, but she told me that she was fine and that I should go to my room and do my homework. I gave her a hug, and just as I thought she was about to break down, I felt her stiffen in my arms before she broke the embrace and went right back to cleaning.

I stayed in my room the rest of the night, and it was torture. I wanted to go and comfort my mom, but I could tell that she felt ashamed and that she wanted to be alone. I barely slept a wink that night and heard Martin coming home at about five in the morning. Mom must have been awake and downstairs when he came in because I could hear them talking in hushed tones. I went down there immediately, just in case he decided to put on a repeat performance. They were standing in the middle of the room hugging, and you could tell that they had both been crying. When he saw me there, he apologized and opened an arm to invite me into the embrace, but I told him, in no uncertain terms, where to go. He was back on the road later that day, so I steered clear until he left.

BK: How long was he gone, and how were things while he was away?

Marie: I remember that his first trip away after that night was one of his shortest in a while and was probably no more than a week. My mom seemed to be back to her old self, and while I tried to bring up the fight with her a couple of times, she always just shrugged it off and steered the conversation elsewhere. She seemed genuinely happy to see Martin when he came home, but her joy was short-lived. He spent that first night home complaining about work and the pressure that he was under, and while he didn't turn any of that negativity on to us, it was still very tense.

Right before bed that night, he came to my room and asked if he could talk to me. I wasn't really about it, but I also knew I couldn't avoid the issue forever, so I let him in. He told me how sorry he was for the way he behaved, but he didn't seem particularly contrite, as most of his speech ended up being about his work and how tired he was all the time. I told him that if I ever saw him lay a hand on my mom again, I would either call the cops or kill him in his sleep, with the latter being the more likely option. That proved to be the conversation stopper for the evening, as he basically mumbled one more apology before hightailing it out of my room.

BK: How did things go after that?

Marie: It felt as though he was really making an effort to get back to being the man he was when he first came into our lives, but you could see that he was struggling to hold it all together. I guess that his job was really stressful and that he was constantly expected to raise the bar and produce bigger and better numbers. In my mind, though, that was just a small part of the problem. I think he enjoyed the jet set life he was leading on the road. He was staying in 5-star hotels and dining like a king every single night, which I assumed made him resent the simple life that he had to return to whenever he landed back in Redfield.

BK: What makes you think that?

Marie: He would generally be a little ornerier when he came home from trips with the other regionals and the big bosses. They would really live it up and go all out on those trips, making it that much tougher to adapt back to a regular life. I'm not saying this to excuse him for his behavior, because the reality is that he was cruel and vindictive towards the end, not to mention violent and dangerous.

BK: Can you tell me a little more about how he would treat your mom when he came back from those trips?

Marie: All I can tell you are secondhand stories that came from my mom. He was very careful to be on his best behavior when I was around. I think the combination of going at him with a knife and threatening to kill him put him on guard around me. I know from the way that I reacted that first time he was abusive that I could absolutely hurt him if it came down to it, and I'm positive that he could tell that I meant what I said and that I would willingly mess him up.

I would see bruises on my mom. Mostly on her arm, so I had an idea that he was getting handsy with her. She would blow it off and say that she was just clumsy, but I knew better. Again, I told her that she needed to get the cops involved if Martin was getting physical, but she said that she could handle him, which she eventually was forced to do.

BK: What was the breaking point for your mom?

Marie: When he choked her out and threatened to kill her. She had become accustomed to his verbal bullshit and his laying hands on her, but the choking crossed the line. I think she had been in a bit of a fog since the dinner table fight, but the choking dispersed the fog and left her with a real sense of clarity. I think it was at that point that mom realized she might actually be in some real danger. She waited until he went to bed that night, then she went upstairs with a baseball bat and gave him some serious whacks, telling him that she was not the only one that should be fearing for their life.

BK: Wow! How did you hear about that?

Marie: Martin told me. He showed me the bruises on his body and had the nerve to suggest that my mom might be coming unhinged. When I asked her about it, mom showed me the marks on her neck where he had gone after her. I called the police that time, but when they came out, neither my mom nor Martin decided to press charges. I told them about all the other stuff he had done, but I knew there was nothing they could do to him at that point given that the only evidence they had to go on was that they were both having a go at each other. The cops did suggest that Martin go stay at a hotel for the night, which is exactly what he did. He was leaving on another business trip the following day, so his bags were already packed and ready to go. He left rather meekly, as the cops stayed around to make sure that he got out of there while he and mom were still both in one piece. It was the last time I ever saw him alive, or fully alive, I should probably say.

BK: Wait, what? Fully alive?

Marie: Yes. He stayed away for a month on that trip. He still called my mom regularly, and she told me that he was dropping hints that he might never come back except to get the rest of his stuff and move on.

BK: How did you mom react to that news?

Marie: Honestly, she seemed relieved. It had become clear to both of us that the man we loved back in the day was gone forever, so it made sense for the man that Martin had become to hitch his wagon and move on. While it was clear that her marriage was dying, mom seemed to take it all in stride. I was getting ready to move out and go to college, and she was thinking about selling and moving out of state. Things at the high school were getting a little weird and tense, and she wanted out.

BK: What was the high school thing all about?

Marie: You'll find out soon enough, I'm guessing. Anyway, I was working a part-time job to make some extra money for college at that point. It was close to the end of the school year, so I would finish my classes and go put in a few hours working as a cashier at the local dollar store. The owner there was pretty strict, though, and had a no cell phone policy, which meant storing your device in a locker in the employee break room. He was cool about letting me study when things were quiet, so it was tough to feel too put out about not being able to get online.

Anyway, on the day when everything went down, I picked up my phone from the locker and saw that there were a ton of missed calls and texts from my mom. They were all essentially saying the same thing, which was that I shouldn't come home right after work. She kept saying that everything was fine, and while she sounded calm enough in the messages, alarm bells were going off in my head.

BK: What did you do?

Marie: I clocked out at work and headed straight home. It wasn't very far from the store to my house, but you better believe that I covered the distance in record time that day. My heart sank when I turned the corner onto our street and saw Martin's car sitting in the driveway. In truth, it was split between the driveway and the lawn with the mailbox sitting smashed beneath the front wheels. Panic sunk in then and I could hardly get the door open. I was shaking like crazy and close to tears, but I knew I had to hold it together as much as possible because I thought I might be stepping into a war zone of sorts.

BK: What was it like once you stepped inside?

Marie: Quiet. I remember it being just too quiet. I wasn't sure whether that was a good thing or a bad thing, but it turned out to be the latter. I called my mom's name but got no response, so I tried calling for Martin, but I had no luck there either. I could hear my blood rushing in my ears, so I forced myself to try and calm down. It was when I got myself under control that I started to hear a tune being hummed. The noise was coming from upstairs, and I could tell that it was my mom who was making it.

I took those stairs two at a time and went to her bedroom, which was where the noise seemed to be coming from. The whole room was trashed, and there was a pool of blood in the middle of the carpet. My mom was still humming that tune. I could tell that the sound was coming from the en suite bathroom, but the blood and the weirdness of the whole scene made it feel as though I was rooted to the spot. I called her name again but got no response. I knew then that I had to go into that bathroom, even though every fiber of my being was telling me to get out and call the cops.

BK: What did you do?

Marie: I dragged myself into the bathroom and then spent the rest of my miserable existence wishing I hadn't. The first thing that hit me was the smell. You read stories about blood and how it has the scent of copper pennies, but it's clear to me now that the people who wrote that have never been in a space soaked in blood and gore. It smelled like days dead roadkill, but there was also the scent of shampoos and soap trying to cut through, making it burn my nostrils like the world's most ineffective potpourri. The stench was truly awful, but I would have gladly taken that if it meant never seeing what caused all that blood.

BK: I know this must be hard, Marie, but can you describe the scene to me?

Marie: Martin was standing in the tub, his hands strapped together with his belt, which was looped around the shower head. I'm not sure that standing is actually the best way to describe his pose, as I'm sure he would have been in a crumpled heap on the porcelain were he not strapped up so tight. My mom was in the tub with him, her back to me, and I could see that she was holding a knife, the very one I went after Martin with all those years previous, and a plunger.

BK: A plunger?

Marie: Uh-huh. She was carving little slices of flesh off his body and stuffing them into his mouth using the wooden handle of the plunger. When she was forcing the meat in, I could see that his front teeth were all essentially shattered and in ruins, probably from the handle being forced into his mouth. Once mom got a chunk in there, she would cover his mouth and try to make him swallow. If that didn't work, she would take the business end of the plunger, place it over his mouth, and hammer away at his face as though she was trying to unplug the toilet. She never once turned around, but she must have heard me come in because she said that she had warned me to stay away and that I should have listened.

I assumed that Martin was dead, but as I turned to run, I saw his eyes roll back into his head, his body twitching as she carved another piece off of his leg. Yes, there were times when I wanted to kill him in those later years, but what mom was doing went way beyond anything that was human.

BK: What did you do when you left the house?

Marie: I called 9-1-1 right away and explained what was happening. They were on scene fast, and they made me get in the back seat of one of the cruisers as they went into the house. They weren't in there for long when I heard shots being fired. They explained to me after the fact that mom wouldn't drop the knife and that they were forced to shoot her when she rushed them, knife still in hand. Martin had breathed his last by that point. There was nothing they could do to bring him back, which is probably for the best given the shape he was in.

BK: What about your mom? Did she survive the shooting?

Marie: She was gone too. These were small-town cops that were on the scene, and they all panicked when she charged. She never had a chance. I can see that you want to ask me more, but that's all there is to tell, so it's time for me to let someone else say their piece.

This Flight Tonight by Eric

Eric: Hey there, writer man. How are you doing? My name is Eric, and I'm ready to tell you my tale.

BK: Thanks, Eric, but can you just give me a moment?

Eric: Sure. Are you alright?

BK: I feel strange. I'm having a hot flash and keep seeing white spots dancing before my eyes. I could really use some water too.

Eric: Hold on, let me go get you a drinky drink of water. I don't have any bottled stuff, so you'll need to settle for what comes out the tap. It can be a little yucky at times, but such is life in a small town.

Author's note: There was a period of about three or four minutes here where the recording continued, although it sounded as though it was nothing but dead air. No background noise, no muted conversation, and no music or singing. Nothing but the sound of my breathing, which, to be honest, sounded a little shallow.

BK: Thanks for that, Eric. Is the water always this color?

Eric: Usually, yeah, but it tastes just fine. Drink up and tell me when you are ready to start.

BK: I'm good, honestly. So, "This Flight Tonight" was your karaoke song. Tell me a little about what that means to you, as well as a little about why you sing it.

Eric: Truth be told, I'm tired of singing it, yet here I am again, belting it out as loud as ever. I suppose it makes sense in some way why it would be in my head given the story I'm about to tell you, but I would sooner get that thing out of there and never hear it again.

BK: So, just stop, Eric. Why keep coming back and putting yourself through the wringer? I want to ask that to everyone I've spoken to. I don't understand what's going on here.

Eric: Drink your water, sit back, and relax, writer man. Each and every one of us here has a story to tell, but we have never sat down and spoken about what happened and why we do the things we do. I don't care about anyone in here but myself, and I would suggest that they all probably feel the same way I do. If you want to try and figure it out once we are all done, you are more than welcome to do so. For now, I just want to say my piece and move on.

BK: This is all so strange, so very strange. Okay, go on then. Where do you want to begin? I'm sure whatever you tell me is going to be brutal, so jump right in wherever you like. This town is fucked.

Eric: Fucked it may be, but it's my town, and it's in my DNA. I was born and raised here, went to school here, got my first job here, and I've never once thought about moving on. If Redfield was good enough for my family when they settled here, then it's sure as shit good enough for me.

BK: Are you telling me, just like all the others, that your family was one of the original settlers in Redfield?

Eric: That's correct. There were eleven families that built homes here and worked the strawberry fields. Once the town started to build up, those families became royalty in these parts. Harold over there even had the high school named after one of his kin. Did he tell you that or was he too modest?

BK: Yes, he told me. I thought he may have been messing with me, though. He seems the type.

Eric: He's a joker, to be sure, but I'd wager that he was on the up and up with everything he dished to you. Listen here, writer man, I'm not trying to be rude or anything, but can we just get to my part in this whole thing?

BK: My apologies. I didn't mean to get you off track. So, you were saying that you were born and raised in Redfield. What was that like?

Eric: I have no complaints. Life here was chill, and I had it pretty good. I was an only child, so my mom doted on me quite a bit. My dad was a pilot with Delta, running international routes, which meant he was gone on a regular basis. When he came home for a stretch, he would always return with something really cool from wherever he had been on his last flight out. My bedroom was filled to brimming with all kinds of cool little trinkets and statues from all over the world. Some of my buddies thought I was a little dorky, but I think they were jealous. I mean, come on, I had the cool dad in town. He drove a little red sports car, and, no, not the Barracuda, and he would come roaring into town still wearing his pilot's uniform. To me, he was the coolest man alive, and I know the other kids thought so as well.

BK: What would you guys get up to when he was home?

Eric: The usual dad and son stuff. We'd go fishing a lot, but if he was really tired and just wanted to chill around the house, he would read to me. He had a huge book collection and was always coming home with two or three new titles at a time. He was the most patient man you ever met in your life. He would read his books aloud, always taking time to answer questions about the bigger words in there, as well as the plotlines that left me a little confused. When I started reading a lot on my own, we would sit side by side with our books, and I would still pester him with questions related to whatever book my face was stuck in at any given time. He didn't seem to mind even though I was probably bugging the ever-loving shit out of him. He would always take time to explain what needed to be explained.

BK: He sounds like a truly wonderful man, Eric.

Eric: He was. The only thing that used to bother him was when I would ask about him taking me up in his plane. He would very calmly explain that it wasn't his plane and how knowing that I was on board would make it tougher for him to concentrate on his job. I would go on and on, begging the way kids always do in hopes of getting their way, but he would shut me down and call it end of discussion. My dad wasn't rude about it; he was simply making it clear that there was no conversation to be had on that subject.

BK: Did he ever decide to take you up?

Eric: He did, but it was very much on his own terms. As a pilot with a big airline, he was basically able to travel anywhere on the cheap whenever he felt like it, plus he got to bring his family along too. I remember him coming home one weekend and not having his usual present for me in tow. I quickly got it into my head that he was mad at me, which was why there was no gift coming, but it was nothing like that at all. He sat me down for a moment and told me that I had a big decision to make. My heart was racing to the point where I thought it was going to come bursting out of my chest and go pinging off all the walls in the house.

BK: How old were you?

Eric: I was just coming up on my tenth birthday. I mean, I was literally a couple of weeks away from heading into double-digits in years, which I believed made me an adult. I may have mentioned that to my dad once or twice, which is why I think he allowed me to make this big decision.

BK: Which was?

Eric: I'm getting there, writer man. Let me revel in this part of the story a little bit. As I was saying, he sits me down and tells me that I have a big decision to make. He says that I need to go into my bedroom, look at all the things that he has brought home for me over the years, and decide which is my favorite. I was thinking that I would just grab the first thing that I saw, and he must have read my mind because he told me to have valid reason why the piece I was selecting was my favorite. I had a couple that I liked, but there was a snow globe that he had brought from Switzerland that I would shake and shake for hours on end.

BK: What was it about the snow globe that you loved so much?

Eric: Being a kid from Georgia, it would be easy to say that it was the snow, but it was more than that. Sure, in the course of my nine years I had never seen as much as a single snowflake, but the truth is that it was the mountains in the snow globe that caught my attention. There was a small village sitting at the bottom of the globe, and I remember thinking that those mountains must have been absolutely massive. I explained this to my dad, telling him what it was I loved about that gift and then asking him if planes could fly high enough to get over those peaks. Some people would have laughed at the stupidity of the question, but not my dad. He explained how he had flown over them countless times and how awesome the Swiss Alps looked from his vantage point.

He took a moment to study the globe, giving it a little shake and watching the snow come down on the mountains and the village below. The anticipation was killing me, but he was so entranced by the falling snow that all I could do was sit and watch him take it all in. By this point, my mom was on the sofa with us, a cheeky grin on her face. Once the last flake of snow settled inside the globe, my dad smiled and asked me if I would like to fly over those mountains with him. I couldn't speak, so I nodded and started crying, noticing that my mom was spilling a few tears of her own. He took my mom's hand as he hugged me and told me that he would be happy to take me, but on his terms.

BK: What did he mean by that?

Eric: We would be going to Switzerland on a family vacation, but he would not be the one flying the plane. I was absolutely fine with that little detail, just as long as I was up in the air with my dad. He told me that he would get everything planned out and that I should be ready to go the day after school ended for the summer. That meant having to wait another couple of weeks, a period of time that I soon convinced myself was going to be torture. It was, but it certainly didn't help that I started packing a bag that very night. I would see that stupid bag sitting at the end of my bed every time I walked into my bedroom, and I swear the clock would tick backward a few seconds every single time.

BK: Ha-ha. That's rough on a kid.

Eric: You're telling me. Anyway, the day before we were due to leave, my dad told me to get my stuff together and take it out to the car. I thought he was just being overly prepared, but it turns out that he had booked us into a fancy hotel close to Hartsfield-Jackson Airport in Atlanta. The room we were in was up on the top floor and had a clear view of the runway. My dad sat with me for what seemed like hours, talking about all the different planes that were taking off, telling me how many passengers they held, how fast they could go, and a ton of other details that I soaked up like a sponge. I didn't want that part to end, but he had booked us into a nice restaurant for dinner, a move that was more for my mom than anything else. She got all gussied up for the occasion, and while I wasn't totally happy about it, I got into dress pants and a shirt with a tie. I thought I looked ridiculous, but when I saw how happy my get-up made my mom, I got over it pretty quick. We had a morning flight out the next day, so the dinner reservations were for earlier than I was used to eating, which felt a little odd. The food was amazing, though, and I ate a ton, all of which made me very sleepy. I think that may have been the plan all along, as I had been shot out of a cannon crazy for the previous two weeks.

BK: Tell me about the day of the flight.

Eric: I was up at the butt crack of dawn, pestering my mom and dad and basically forcing them out of bed before they were really ready to get the day started. Luckily, it was only a few short hours before we had to head to the airport, so they were able to get me under control and ready to roll in no time at all. My dad told me to save all my questions for the flight, saying that it would be easier to answer them all once we were on board and ready to take off. He had a pre-flight checklist made up for me, which certainly helped me calm down.

BK: What was on the list?

Eric: Nothing of any real importance. It was all little tasks designed to ensure that I stayed busy over the next couple of hours. It was things like brushing my teeth, eating a full breakfast, making sure that my favorite toys were in the carryon bag and other things of that nature. It was all very trivial stuff, but it made me feel like I was the most important kid in the world. My mom and dad were great at that type of thing and were able to instill a lot of confidence in me at an early age without turning me into an obnoxious little shit.

Once we got to the airport, we were able to skip the security line and get right through. We were also allowed on the plane ahead of everyone, giving my mom time to sit and relax while my dad introduced me to the captain and gave me a little tour of the cockpit. One thing I remember as being odd about the visit was that my dad seemed to bristle when he saw the pilot. He was a man that got along with everyone, so it was weird to see the tension between him and the captain. I've replayed that entire day in my head countless times, but it wasn't until I got older that the weirdness between those two registered with me.

BK: What was it all about? Did your dad ever tell you?

Eric: We didn't talk much about that day in the years following, but when I asked my dad outright if I was imagining the tension, he filled me in on the details. I'll get to that in a minute since it might help explain what went down. I was still incredibly excited to be on board, but that quickly turned to fear once we started backing away from the gate. The plane had been quiet and calm up to that point, but once we got moving, it felt as though I was trapped inside the belly of a big, hungry beast that was growling and generally acting pissed off. Sensing that I was about to flip out, my dad took my hand and started talking me through all the different sounds. It took him a minute, but I did eventually calm down, and once we started barreling down that runway, I was back to being giddy again.

The first couple of hours of the flight were uneventful, and I think I might even have slept for a while. I had initially been sitting in the middle seat, but I asked my mom if she would let me sit by the window for a little while. She was happy to oblige, letting me scooch over so that I could get a look at the clouds floating below us, seeming to move ever so slowly in spite of how fast the plane was going. I became transfixed on those clouds, looking for animals and other shapes hidden in the fluffy masses. I might have stayed that way for the rest of the flight had I and the rest of the passengers on the plane not been distracted by a loud booming noise.

BK: Did one of the engines go out?

Eric: Yeah, that's what I found out later. After the initial boom, there was a high-pitched whining sound and the plane tilted off to the left, which is the side that I was sitting on. I pulled down the plastic blind on the window, as it felt as though we were going sideways towards the ground, but we probably didn't drop down that much. I looked at my dad and saw that he was gripping the armrests on the seat, muttering to himself as he looked at the cockpit door. The whining started to get even louder, and the plane started rocking from side to side. I was terrified by that point and was snuggled up against my mom. I could hear and feel her heart pounding, so even as she was trying to soothe me, I could tell that she was scared too. Over the noise of the plane, I could hear my dad still muttering, only he was getting louder and easier to hear. He was alternating between saying "correct the bird" and "make an announcement," and seemed to get angrier when neither was happening.

BK: How long did this go on for?

Eric: I honestly don't know, but I can tell you that it felt like an eternity. Passengers were starting to scream and cry, and I heard more than a few people praying. One of the flight attendants went into the cockpit, and when she came back out, she looked terrified. You could she was trying to hold it together for the passengers, but she was scared. That was when my dad took action. We were sitting just behind the first-class section, so he was up at the cockpit door in a matter of a few strides. He spoke to the flight attendant, who I guess he knew, and she let him into the cockpit. I only caught a glimpse, but the co-pilot looked as though he was out cold, while the captain was sitting there doing nothing. The door slammed shut right after my dad stepped inside, and it felt as though the plane returned to normal a few short moments after that.

BK: I'm guessing your dad took control.

Eric: He did, but it was a struggle to do so. It turns out that the captain of the flight had been suspended by the airline a couple of years earlier. There had been rumors of him drinking before flights and of having some issues with depression and anxiety. He was frequently tested for alcohol before flying, but he always passed with flying colors. Still, many of the flight attendants and co-pilots that he worked with complained about his behavior, to the point where Delta took action and grounded him, forcing him to seek some professional help. He was cleared to fly shortly before our trip, which explains why my dad was a little surprised to see him there.

BK: What happened in the cockpit?

Eric: My dad didn't go into too much detail, but the official investigation was released to the public and told quite the tale. After the engine blew, the captain totally froze and appeared not to know what to do. When the co-pilot tried to take over the controls, the captain socked him and told him not to touch his plane, all the while still doing nothing to get the situation under control. It seems that the flight attendant walked in just as the violent part was going down. The reports said that my dad had to physically remove the captain from the seat so that he could get in and get the plane back under control. I had stopped looking after my dad left, and I had my face buried in my mom's chest. It seems that there was an off-duty air marshal on board. He was called into the cockpit to restrain the captain until we were diverted and landed safely.

BK: What happened after that? Did you and your parents continue with your holiday as planned?

Eric: No. That whole incident seemed to suck the life out us, and we just wanted to go home. My dad was stuck giving statements for a few hours after we had our emergency landing. Once he was done, Delta arranged for a private jet to take us back to Atlanta. Let me tell you, the thrill of flying had left me by that point. I spent the whole flight back home in a state of frozen panic. It was the last time I ever set foot on a plane.

BK: Well, it's nice to hear that it all ended so well, but given what the rest of the people here have told me up until now, I have a feeling that your story is not quite over.

Eric: You are very astute, writer man. There certainly is a little more to my story, although it is perhaps not as grim as some of the others that you will have heard already. It may not register as high on the horror scale as the others, but it leaves me in pain every time I think about it.

BK: I'm more than happy to let it go. What you have already told me fits the song nicely enough, so if you don't want to tell it, I'm seriously okay with that.

Eric: That's not really an option at this point. I don't believe in leaving things unfinished, so let's just soldier on and get to the rest of it. The telling hurts like hell, but that's a pain that I live with all the time. So, shall I continue?

BK: Um, yes.

Eric: Life returned to normal, for the most part, once we got back to Redfield, but my dad was home permanently from that point forward. He had become a bit of a media darling after news of the incident got out, and while Delta was keen on rolling him out as some kind of hero, he wasn't interested. He decided to retire and received a very nice settlement that was more than enough to keep us living comfortably. He already had a decent nest egg socked away prior to that. I guess I forgot to mention that my dad was a little older than the other fathers of kids my age. He had been laser-focused on getting his pilot's license and building his career before settling down to marry and start a family. There was a 15-year age difference between my mom and dad, but he always seemed a whole lot younger than he was. After that flight, he seemed more than happy to put his career behind him and spend time hanging out with mom and me, but it didn't last.

BK: He became bored?

Eric: Yes, but not with his life with us. Flying was always an adrenaline rush for my dad, and he missed the high that he got from being up and over the world. He wasn't interested in going back to commercial flying, but he had an idea that he could start his own business, so he invested in a crop duster. We were surrounded by farmland, yet none of the land owners ever thought to spray their fields this way, choosing instead to go the old-fashioned route. They all claimed that it was too expensive to go with a crop-dusting plane, but my father made them an offer they couldn't refuse. He wasn't interested in making a buck off his neighbors. For him, it was more about getting back up in the air, so he charged the bare minimum required to keep that bad boy flying. Whenever there was any type of mechanical issue with the plane, Neil would come by and work his magic, getting that old bird up and running again.

Our house sat on a big bit of land, plenty big enough for him to build an airstrip and a hangar. The local farmers loved the new set-up. The crop duster saved them time and money, both of which they viewed as valuable commodities. Crops blossomed, the farmers made more money, and they tried to cut my dad in on their profits, but he just wasn't interested. For him, it was all about the flying. Whenever he got done with the spraying, he would do a little fly-by over the house, maneuvering the plane so that it looked as though it was waving at us. I would hear the plane coming and run out onto the porch so that I could see him give that little wave before he landed.

BK: That's a nice memory.

Eric: Yes, but it's tainted now. The last day I saw him was just like every other. He ate his breakfast, spent some time talking to me about my day, gave my mom a kiss and a hug, and then left, telling me to listen for him coming back so that he could give me the wave. That day, I heard the plane coming a whole lot earlier than usual. I didn't think anything of it, assuming that he was cutting out early to come home, which he did every now and again. I ran out to the porch and waited for him to fly over, but I could tell right away that something wasn't right. The plane was sputtering and making noises I had never heard it make before. When he flew over the house, he was doing the wave maneuver, but you could tell he was fighting the movement as opposed to controlling it. Worst of all, the spraying mechanism was still doing its thing, shooting a fine mist of red liquid in the wake of the plane. The spray fell on the house, staining the white siding and spattering against the kitchen window.

I'm not sure if it was the noise of the plane or the pesticide hitting the house that brought my mom outside, but she came tearing out onto the porch, her hands still dripping wet from washing dishes in the kitchen sink. I heard her say something about blood before she caught sight of the plane, which was now looking seriously out of control. She let out a piercing scream at that point, a sound so piercing it raised gooseflesh across my entire body. Her scream was loud, but it was soon drowned out with the sound of the plane smashing into the town water tower. The booming noise it made reminded me of the one I heard on the plane to Switzerland, but I knew this one was going to be a whole lot worse, and I was right.

BK: I'm sorry, Eric. I really don't know what to say. Your dad didn't make it?

Eric: No, it was total carnage downtown, although the high school got the worst of it, other than my dad, of course.

BK: What happened with the school?

Eric: I only heard little bits and pieces, so I'm not the best person to tell that part of the story. Norm was the janitor at the school, and he was there the day of the crash. I'm sure he will unhappily fill you in on all the details.

School's Out by Norm

BK: Hello, Norm. I hope we have time to have this conversation since it looks as though closing time is upon us.

Norm: Where the heck would you get that idea?

BK: The overhead lights are getting turned up. I've been to enough bars in my time to know that's usually a sign that the end of the night is coming.

Norm: Still looks the same in here to me. The boss is in charge of all the bigger stuff. He hasn't told me nothing except that I should come and talk to you. Seems as though he has taken a bit of a shine to you, since he's told us all to come and have a jawing session.

BK: Can I talk to the boss once we get done?

Norm: That's entirely up to him and it ain't got nothing to do with me. If he wants to sit awhile, he'll let you know in his own good time. The question now, though, is what it is that you want from me.

BK: Well, I don't know how much you know about why I'm here. I operate…

Norm: I know why you're here; I need to know which part of my story you are interested in. There are some juicy parts throughout, some of which might help you start piecing together the other things that you have heard tonight. My guess is that, as a writer, you want all the little warts and blemishes included unless, of course, you plan on taking what you are told and getting all creative with it.

BK: Given what I've heard to this point, Norm, I don't believe I could get any more creative. It's been a bit of a horror show, to be honest, and while I'm reaching the end of my rope, I get a sense that I haven't heard the whole story. There are loose ends and inconsistencies all over.

Norm: I'm not sure how many of those loose ends will be pieced together for you here, but what I can do is give you my part and let you do with it what you will. Even if you do get creative and start messing around with the details, I'll never find out. I'm not planning on reading anything you write. You know that old saying about the truth being stranger than fiction? I think that applies to our town.

BK: I believe you, Norm, I truly do, so let's get to it. Let's forget about the song and just jump right into your time in Redfield. How does that sound?

Norm: Works for me. Now, where to begin? I'm a little different from the rest of this group in that I wasn't born here, but I have lived most of my life in Redfield. By most, I mean all but the few days I spent in hospital in Atlanta after I was born. Shortly after my momma dropped me out of the womb, she went for a walk and never did bother coming back. I was destined to be put into the system and left to rot, but that's not how things played out for me. I don't know the full story of how I ended up with the Ramsey family, but given that I was born around the same date as my half-brother Peter, my guess is that some sort of deal was struck at the hospital to get me out of there and into a loving family. I never knew any family other than the Ramsey's, so I loved them as you would your own, all except for Peter. Me and him never did see eye to eye.

BK: What was the problem with Peter?

Norm: From the moment we were old enough to communicate, he made it clear that he was none too happy with me being part of the family. That boy was born with an air of superiority, and he would often tell me how the Ramsey family was one of the original founders of Redfield and how my blood wasn't pure enough to live up to the family name. He was constantly trying to get under my skin, and while it sure did hurt, I never let him see that he was getting to me. I figured that if I ignored his taunts, they would stop, but he kept right on trying to annoy me, almost as if he were trying to goad me into a fight. I'm sure that he believed that if I lashed out and hit him, I would be banished back to wherever I came from. Life was too good for me to fall into that trap.

BK: He sounds like an asshole.

Norm: Oh, he was a whole lot worse than that, let me tell you. He was an entitled little shit, but his mean streak was creepier in that he was able to switch it off and on at will. Momma and Poppa thought the sun shined out of his ass because he was always as sweet as pie around them, but when they turned their backs, you could see the light go out of his eyes and the darkness sweep in. He annoyed me when we were young uns', but as we got older, that annoyance turned into fear. That boy was a sociopath, straight up.

BK: What makes you say that besides the way he treated you?

Norm: It was the way he treated everyone, not just me. It was as though he was born without any kind of emotion, other than hate, or empathy. He read books about murderers and serial killers, and he had a weird obsession with the very worst parts of history. He had zero friends at school, at least not that I saw, and he would sit in the lunchroom and survey the scene with a blank expression on his face. He would have probably been picked on had everyone not been totally terrified of him.

BK: Did he do something that made people fear him so?

Norm: He didn't have to. He had this weird aura around him that acted as a shield of sorts. People didn't want to be anywhere near him, and no-one ever thought about fucking with him. Imagining the things that he could do was a whole lot worse than anything he could have done, or so we all thought, so people let him brood and wallow in his own weirdness.

BK: What about the teachers and other adults? How did he interact with them?

Norm: The very same way he behaved around my parents. He was a straight A student and never got into any kind of trouble. If a teacher needed help or called on someone in class, he was always the first to get involved. They all loved him, and they all failed to see what the kids saw. In fairness, he made it easy for them to be blinded to who he really was.

BK: But you saw him, right?

Norm: Man, I saw right through him, although his varnished veneer disappeared around me. He made no effort to hide who he was when I was with him. Honestly, I think he was taunting me and trying to get me to say something to Momma and Poppa, even when we got older and were beyond the point of me getting sent away to some shitty orphanage. I knew that the time would eventually come when I wouldn't need to be in his life, but he made that change, made me realize that I always needed to be around to keep an eye on him.

BK: That seems a little too calculated even for someone as off as he sounds. What happened that made you feel that way?

Norm: It was the night that poor woman got hit by the car. We saw the whole thing go down, and before you ask, no, we never saw who was driving. The cops grilled us about that for hours, but the glass on the car was as black as coal. You couldn't see shit, and I honestly don't know how the driver was able to see out.

When she went flying over the car and snapped her legs on the landing, I can honestly say it was the only time in my life where I saw Peter look genuinely happy, but that wasn't the worst of it. The moment she hit the ground, he wheeled around and grabbed me by the arm, yelling "DID YOU SEE THAT?" after which he let out this weird cowboy yeehaw. I pushed him away and asked what the fuck was wrong with him, which was when I noticed that he had a hard-on. He was giddy as all get out, but he took on a somber tone when the cops arrived on the scene. I think he might even have cried in front of them. I knew then that he was more messed up than I thought, but he really made it obvious once he picked up a part-time job at the barbershop.

BK: What happened then?

Norm: We were about sixteen years old when he applied for that job. The help wanted sign was taken down about two minutes after he went in to talk to the owner. Like I said, he had all the adults fooled and wrapped around his little finger. He came strutting into the house that day, proud as punch, and loudly declaring that he was a working man now. I swear, if you didn't know him the way I did, you would have thought him to be the most charming kid in the world. It was frightening the way he was able to switch it off and on.

So, he took that job and never missed a single day. It was nothing more than grunt work, sweeping up hair and making coffee for the barbers. Still, he was a daily fixture at work, even on days when he wasn't scheduled to be there. He would work for free, which I thought was very strange until I found out what he was doing. It was…damn, this is tough to put out there.

BK: We can take a break. I'm more than happy to get off this discussion.

Norm: No. This story has to be told. Okay, so, we shared a bedroom, which was not very pleasant for me given that I thought Peter might snap at any given moment. Momma and Poppa always talked about putting an extension on the home, but they never got around to it. I believe they thought that Peter and me were the best of friends and that we enjoyed our shared space. It reached a point where I simply didn't have the heart to tell them what their son really was, but the thing with the hair almost made me break my vow of silence.

BK: Hair? I'm really not so sure that I want to hear any more of this.

Norm: Let me go talk to the boss and see what he says.

Authors note: Another few minutes passed while Norm was apparently away talking. Again, the only sound heard on the recording at that time was my breathing, which was beginning to sound rather ragged.

Norm: The boss says that he would like for you to stay a little while longer. He says he'll talk to you when you have heard from all of us.

BK: How many more?

Norm: The boss says that there is just one more after me, at which point he will sit with you and tell you his story. Can you hang in there?

BK: I guess so. I suppose you had better tell me about the hair then.

Norm: Like I was saying, Peter and me shared the same room, and there were times when I would hear him shuffling around at night. Being so close to him made me a very light sleeper, so I was aware of all his movements, although I couldn't ever really pinpoint what the hell he was up to. He became even more active at night after landing the job in the barbershop. I started hearing what sounded like a lock being rattled, so I took it upon myself to search our room one day when he was at work. He had a small lockbox hidden under his bed, but it was protected by a big padlock, which is what I assumed he was messing with at night. I wanted to bust that thing open, but I was also afraid to see what was inside and what he would do to me when he found it broken. Instead, I decided to pretend I was asleep that night and keep an eye on what he was doing.

BK: Jesus, I'm not so sure I want to hear this.

Norm: Sorry, but it's part of the story. I was expecting a bit of a long haul that night, but I heard him get up and start fiddling with the lock about an hour after lights out. I stayed as still as possible, not wanting to alert him to the fact that I was awake, although I felt as though my breathing was loud enough to wake the dead. He didn't appear to notice though, as he went about his business as usual. The rattling with the lock was over in no time, after which I heard this weird crinkling sound that seemed to be keeping perfect rhythm with his heavy breathing. Curiosity was killing me, so I jumped up, flipped on my bedside light, and then wished that I had just gone to sleep as usual.

Given what was going on, it's probably odd to say that the first thing I noticed was the open lockbox sitting on the floor. It was full to brimming with Ziploc bags filled with hair. Each of the bags had a name written in Sharpie on the front, as well as a date filled in below the name. It was serial killer stuff, but rather than focusing on one type or hair color or gender, he had a little bit of everything. I felt sick to my stomach, but the bile really started to rise when I saw what Peter was doing. He was laying on his bed, huffing on a bag of hair and having a real good go at himself if you know what I mean. The worst part of it all is that he was staring right at me as he hammered away.

BK: What the hell did you do?

Norm: I ran out the room and made it to the toilet just in time before I threw up everything that I had eaten for the past month. Momma came out to check on me, as I guess I was loud enough to wake her up. I was weak-kneed and trembling by the time I was done, and even though I assured her that I was okay, she insisted on helping me back to my room. I didn't want her to see Peter going cuckoo, but I also thought that she might be able to get him some help if she could see for herself that he wasn't right. None of it mattered, though, because his side of the room was neat and tidy, and he was lightly snoring under the covers of his bed. It was at that point that I started to think that maybe I had imagined the whole thing, that maybe I had eaten something bad and was suffering from the effects of that. I never could fully convince myself of that idea though, as I continued to hear him doing his business in our room most nights from that day forward.

BK: How were you able to maintain your cool in that house knowing what he was up to? I think I might have gone nuts.

Norm: I knew he was leaving soon. He had been accepted to the University of Georgia with the goal of becoming a teacher, which struck me as an odd profession for someone who didn't seem to care about anyone but himself. I didn't spend too much time thinking about it though, as the thought of getting him out of the house for a few years was incredibly appealing.

BK: Did you go to college? You certainly sound smart enough, yet I am told that you are a janitor.

Norm: My grades were just okay. I graduated high school, but I really didn't do well enough to get into a decent school. I was okay with that though, as Momma had become quite sick in our senior year. Poppa did his best, but he wasn't really handy around the house. He needed help, and I was more than happy to lend a hand in any way that I could. By the time Momma got better, I was pretty much settled in Redfield, working odd jobs here and there and never settling too long in one place. I had a little bit of money in my pocket and was happier with Peter gone, so life seemed to be as good as it was going to get.

BK: How did you end up in the janitorial position in the high school?

Norm: It was Peter's return to Redfield that led me to Haskins High. When he graduated from UGA, he announced that his dream was to teach high school in his hometown. He said that he had been afforded certain privileges by being part of one of the original families and that he wanted to give back to the community. It all smelled like bullshit to me, but I will say that he seemed like a changed man when he came home. The darkness seemed to have fled his eyes, and he seemed genuinely happy to be back in Redfield. Damn, he was even civil to me, perhaps for the very first time in his life. The school was in desperate need of a new English teacher with the new school year fast approaching, and while Peter was overqualified for the position, he willingly took it on. As the start of the school year got closer, I could see some of the old Peter start to creep back in, as though he was split again. I'm of the belief that a residue of shit gets left behind when something awful happens in a place, and given what has gone down in Redfield, it stands to reason that Peter would breathe it in and rediscover his wicked self.

BK: You make it sound as though he was possessed.

Norm: That makes sense to me. He absorbed the negativity of this town, and it made him bad. I'm not suggesting that he wasn't off from the beginning, because he obviously was, but returning to this town is what did him in. When the janitor job came open at the school, I decided to take it so that I could keep an eye on him. Obviously, I couldn't watch him at all times, but I could be close if he decided to do anything crazy.

BK: You were looking to protect your brother?

KARAOKE NIGHT

Norm: What? Have you lost your mind? Have you not been listening to what I've been saying about him? No, I was not there to protect my brother. I was there to take him down if he did anything to the kids he was teaching. I'm the only one who knew what he really was, which meant that everyone else he came into contact with was potentially in danger. Look, as far as I knew, he had never done anything to harm someone physically, but you have to keep in mind that I had no idea what he was capable of doing, but the longer he was back in town, the more he looked dead in the eyes. He had left his lockbox behind when he left for Atlanta, but it disappeared after one of his visits, probably into the house that he rented after he returned home. I mean, was he going to be happy with his hair collection or was he looking to upgrade? I wasn't about to sit around and wait for that answer to come from a cop via a coroner's report.

BK: Okay, Norm, I get it. So, how did things go with him at the school? Was he able to control himself?

Norm: He instantly became the goddamn teacher of the century. Every kid in his class saw their grades steadily start to climb, plus he was involved in all kinds of different after-school activities and fundraisers. People saw him as a saint, except maybe for the kids. I would always take a moment to peek into his classroom while I was mopping the halls and was always stunned at how quiet and attentive his kids were compared to other classes. They all had this vacant stare thing going on when he talked. It was like, it was, you know how they say that kids can see ghosts and demons and shit before they are conditioned to believe that it's all bullshit?

BK: Yes.

Norm: It was like that, like they saw him for what he really was, but it didn't quite fully register. They were in the same position as I was in that they couldn't say anything about him. They were getting good grades, and that was all that the parents cared about. The problem, though, was that a couple of them were starting to act out a little outside of school. Craig Black was the first to become a problem child. He was a quiet kid, grade A student, and all-around good guy, but a couple of months in the presence of my brother changed all that. He developed a mean streak and became the school bully. Things eventually got really bad with him, even after Peter was gone. I'm guessing my brother must have got his hooks in that boy in a big way. The other kids who were under his spell seemed to snap out of it once he died, but not Craig.

BK: Does the plane crash that Eric was talking about have something to do with your brother's demise?

Norm: It certainly did, and it almost got me too. We ended up with a hostage situation in the school that day, but I should probably fill you in, as best I can, on how we reached that point. It was the second to last day of the school year, so only about half of the kids had shown up. All the important business had been taken care of, so no-one was going to bust their balls for skipping the last couple of days. Some of the parents were keeping their kids out because things were starting to get a little weird. One teacher had already slaughtered her husband, and the rumor mill was starting to go into high gear in regards to my brother. He was always affectionate with his kids, hugging them and generally just being handsy, although not in a way that initially aroused suspicion in anyone. It was when he was caught sniffing their hair that things took a turn. When confronted by one of the parents, he laughed it off and basically accused the parent of being paranoid. He turned on the charm again with that conversation, making everyone believe that he was the salt of the earth. Peter was a lot more careful around the kids after that though, but I was watching, and I saw him doing the hair smelling thing. I should have gone to the cops before I did, although choosing not to meant that my brother was taken out of the picture permanently, so not a totally awful decision.

BK: When did you eventually talk to them?

Norm: On the day he holed up in the school with a kid that was threatening to blow the whistle on Peter's weirdness. This kid had just moved to town a month earlier and seemed immune to the spell that my brother was casting. I have a theory about that. Peter seemed to be returning to the way he was after he first came back from Atlanta. It was as though whatever evil shit was inside him was being transferred to the kids, like a demon jumping from one possessed body to another. He was getting better, I could see it, but he wasn't quite fully there yet when it all went down in the school that day. I guess Peter and the new kid got into it in the classroom, with the student saying that he was going to get my brother sent to jail. A scuffle ensued, which sent some of the kids running out of the room. I'm told that Craig Black was standing on his desk yelling at Peter to kill the kid and that he tossed a knife in their direction as his classmates dragged him out. The cops had been called by them, and no-one wanted to get caught in the potential crossfire. Someone pulled the fire alarm, which sent the few remaining folks, myself included, running for the door. It wasn't until I got outside that I was filled in on what was happening.

BK: What did you do?

Norm: The cops were on me right quick, telling me that my brother had a knife pressed to a kid's neck inside his classroom. They were looking to me for a way to talk him down, hoping that I would know how to get through to him. It was then that I told them about the lockbox and how I've always believed him to be a little off. You could feel everything change at that point, as it became clear that the cops wanted blood. They got plenty of that, but just not in the way they were expecting.

BK: What do you mean?

Norm: Shut up and listen, man. Peter's classroom was on the bottom floor, and there were about twenty cops with their guns trained on him, ready to pull the trigger if they got a clear shot. I'm not sure how he managed it, but Peter had picked me out in the crowd and was staring me down. He looked scared to me, which was something I had never seen him be before. No-one was paying me any attention at that point, so I ran back into the school and made a beeline for his classroom. He was still looking out the window when I arrived, but he knew I was there just the same.

I told him to back up and come to the door, which he did. The kid was screaming at me to help him, but my full attention was on my brother. I figured if I could keep him cool and calm and get him to drop the knife, we might all get out of this alive. He made it all the way to the door, dragging the kid with him and keeping the point of the knife pressed against the boy's neck. There was a little trickle of blood running down and staining the collar of the kid's white shirt. I could see the veins in his neck standing out because of how tightly Peter was grabbing hold of him, and I knew that too much pressure on one of those veins with the blade of the knife was going to create a real problem. I put my hand on Peter's shoulder, feeling him flinch under my touch, and I spoke as softly as I could, telling that he needed to give me the knife, let the kid go, and come outside with me. He turned his head to the side then, tucking in behind the kid, almost as if he knew he was in the crosshairs. There were tears spilling down his cheek, and he looked like a scared little boy. He told me he was sorry for everything as he handed me the knife. I was sure that the cops could see it all going down from their vantage point, so I pulled Peter and the kid out into the hallway so they wouldn't have a clear shot, which was right about the time we heard the noise.

BK: What noise? Was it the plane?

Norm: It sounded like a wounded animal baying in pain. I wasn't hanging around waiting to see what it was, so I grabbed the kid's arm and headed for the exit, yelling at Peter to come with us. He shook his head and stepped back inside the classroom, the sound of the bullets tearing through the glass competing with the sound of the plane, which was getting steadily louder. I knew that he was gone as soon as I heard them start shooting, so my sole focus now was on getting the kid out of there.

As soon as we set foot outside, it was obvious that the plane was heading in our direction. It was the crop duster that we had all become used to seeing fly overhead, but you could tell it was in trouble, and it was heading our way. The kid pulled himself free from my grip and took off towards the cops out in the parking lot. That seemed liked a pretty solid idea to me, so I went right after him, just as the plane flew over, dumping shit all over all of us before crashing into the water tower. I threw myself down on the ground, bracing for an explosion that never came. There was a loud bang, but not the hellfire that you might expect. That said, the force of the impact was enough to send the water tower teetering to one side, where it hung, seemingly suspended for a moment, before crashing down on top of the school. Bricks and chunks of metal came cascading down in a mini tidal wave, but no-one was seriously hurt, although a few did have some cuts and bruises that needed attending to.

BK: That must have been some cleanup job. Did they recover the body of your brother and the pilot?

Norm: It took weeks to clear the area, but yes, they got the bodies out, including one that was unexpected.

BK: Was there another kid trapped in the school at the time of the crash?

Norm: No, this one was in the pesticide tank of the plane. It was the body of a headless child. Word was that it was badly decomposed due to being mixed with the chemicals. The plane had been spraying blood and little niblets of flesh along with the pesticide, with the assumption being that the potent mix clogged up the works and somehow messed with the controls. I don't know about everyone else, but I spent days in the shower after that little revelation, although some stains never wash off even though they aren't visible to the naked eye.

BK: Wait. A headless child? Was it Calvin? You know, the kid whose body went missing during the tornado?

Norm: There wasn't really enough left to identify it properly, but the general consensus was that it was indeed that boy. Now, if you'll excuse me,

I need to go report to the boss and let him know that it's almost his time to talk.

Love Shack by Tanya

Tanya: Hello there. Are you still with us?

BK: Please stop snapping your fingers in my face. I just need to close my eyes for a second. I'm exhausted by all of this. None of this is what I was after. I just wanted to do a small piece about dive bars and then go home. This is all too much.

Tanya: Sometimes we get more than we bargained or asked for. It's really that simple. You stumbled into something unexpected, but what a story you'll have to tell when all is said and done, right?

BK: It seems I don't have a choice here. I'd get up and leave, but I know that I'm too tired to drive, and I am genuinely interested in what the boss has to say. I've seen him looking over here several times during these talks, and he looks like the cat that got the cream. Enough about him. I'm Brian. What's your name, and what is it that you have for me?

Tanya: A pleasure to make your acquaintance, Brian. My name is Tanya, and like everyone else here, I have a story to tell. It's stories that you were after, isn't that the case?

BK: Not like this. I only wanted to know about connections to the songs.

Tanya: Isn't that what you are getting? I understand that the subject matter may not tickle your fancy, but you are getting exactly what you asked for. I'll warn you in advance, Brian, I may be a pretty young country girl, but I am not going to sugarcoat the details of my story to make you happy. That's not how this works. You ask the questions, and I'll give the answers, all tied up with a pretty pink ribbon on top.

BK: Go on then. Tell your twisted story, but before we begin, can you answer me one simple question? Why is it so bright in here?

Tanya: It's not that bright, Brian. I'll do what I can to be a sweet girl and get the story out as quickly as possible. I'm more than just a pretty face, you know, which is why all the men in town wanted to be with me, at least until SHE came along.

BK: Who are you referring to when you say "she?"

Tanya: The boss has all the details on that bitch, but I'll do what I can to give you my side of how things went down and how she fucked up my life. I'm sorry. I know girls shouldn't swear, but she was a big pain in my behind, that one.

BK: What did she do to you that made you hate her so?

Tanya: It's a little tough to explain, so I'm going to need to break my promise and go all the way back to the beginning. This might take a little longer than expected, but it will help put everything into context for you. Are you okay with that, sweetie?

BK: Tanya, as much as I appreciate your going into detail for me, I'd just as soon you give me the short version.

Tanya: Oh, don't be like that. Do you really want to sit and watch me be all pouty and sulky while I talk, or would you rather see me happy and beautiful? The last choice is the better one, I promise.

BK: At this point, I really don't care.

Tanya: Now you've gone and hurt my feelings, just like every man I know. I thought you were nicer than that, I really did.

BK: You are quite the manipulator, Tanya. What with that sweet demeanor and beauty queen affect, you should be in the movies. I am a nice man, by the way; I'm just no longer in the mood to be messed with. Tell the whole story if you must, Tanya, but knock off the pretty girl persona. I imagine we'll get through this quicker if you go that route.

Tanya: Fine, have it your way, but there's no need to be rude about it.

BK: It wasn't my intention…

Tanya: Hush up and let's get this over with. Let me just say that it's funny you should mention me being a beauty queen because everyone always said that I should go to the pageant circuit. I would have, too, if I hadn't been raised by my grandpa. He was a lot of things, but assistant to the stars was certainly not one of them. If you think about it, though, he was a minor celebrity of sorts, at least in these parts. He could provide things that you don't normally find in a small town.

BK: Such as?

Tanya: I'm getting to that part, mister impatient. Let a girl gather her thoughts so I can tell this the right way. Damn, now I'm making myself sound like the typical dumb blonde, which you should know that I am not. Like I was saying, I lived in a big old house with my grandpa, the very one he built when he established this town alongside the other families. He was always very good with his hands, but he was even better with his mouth, as he could sell ice to an Eskimo, not that there was ever any ice around these parts.

BK: Okay, now let's just stop here for a moment. You look to be no more than nineteen or twenty to me, yet here you are ready to spin some yarn about life down on the farm with your dear old grandpappy, who just happened to be among the first folk in Redfield. Tanya, not to be insulting, but I am calling bullshit on you and everyone else in this shithole establishment. Yes, you have all kept me entertained, but the pieces don't fit together in what you are all telling me. I'm tired, I'm hungry and thirsty, I have a blinding headache, and I just want to get the fuck out of Dodge. Why the hell are you crying?

Tanya: This is so very unfair. All I want to do is tell my story and make the boss happy. He said...

Unknown: It looks as though it might be time for me to intervene here. Tanya, stay where you are and let me sort this out with Mr. Keane, okay, sweetheart?

Tanya: Yes, sir.

Unknown: Brian, I understand that you are not very happy right now and that you want to leave, but I am asking that you stay just a little while longer. Tanya here has been very patient in waiting her turn to talk, and while I get that she can be a little much to take when you don't feel great, I still believe in treating a lady right, which is why I ask that you hear her out.

BK: Oh, the big boss man speaks. It's about time you introduced yourself, although you haven't even done that properly.

Unknown: My name is (garbled), and I am more than just the boss here, I am the owner operator. You are in my territory now, Mr. Keane, and while I can very easily make you stay and listen until we are all done here, I would rather that you did so of your own volition. Whaddya say, champ? You ready to stick it out a while longer?

BK: Will I get to have a sit-down conversation with you once she's done?

Unknown: You have my word on that, Mr. Keane. Now, here are some strawberries and some more water to tide you over, maybe help you get a little pep back in your step.

BK: Thank you.

Unknown: My pleasure. Now, can you please resume your chat with Tanya? Look how distraught the poor little creature is. Her makeup is running, and everything, which I can tell you will drive her nuts.

Tanya: May I take a moment to compose myself and freshen up, sir?

Unknown: No, you may not, Tanya. Mr. Keane's time is valuable, so it is perhaps best that you get back to your story and get it told, like a good girl. Can you do that for me?

Tanya: Yes, sir.

Unknown: Excellent, then I'll leave you both to it. We shall speak soon, Mr. Keane.

BK: Please don't cry, Tanya, and please accept my apologies for being such an ass. I am tired and confused, but that's not your fault. At least, I don't think it is. I still get the feeling that I am being played, but I did come here to listen, so I'll shut up and do that.

Tanya: See, I was right after all. You are a nice man. I must look a mess.

BK: You look lovely, Tanya.

Tanya: You sure know how to flatter a girl, but I'll take your word for it. Now, what was I talking about before? Oh, right, I was talking about growing up with my grandpa, with the strawberry fields growing out back beyond the big barn where grandpa spent a lot of his free time. He made it very clear that I was not allowed in the barn, telling me that there were things in there that no little girl should be privy to. I eventually found out what he was up to in there, but only when he granted me permission to step inside and become part of the family business.

BK: Someone made mention of a moonshine man earlier tonight. Was it your grandfather that they were talking about?

Tanya: Yes, it was, but he was more than just the liquor man in town. He could get you just about anything you asked for, which is probably why we always had a steady stream of visitors stopping by our place. I was still a little girl when he started wheeling and dealing, but I soon learned that being pretty sure had its benefits. A lot of the men would bring me candy, which they would hand over after I did a song and dance routine for them. Some of those men would bellow with laughter, while others would go a bit quiet and look at me in a way that made me feel funny inside. Some of them scared me, but I forgot all about that when I got the candy, and some of them would even give me a nickel. I had an old mason jar in my bedroom where I saved my money. When I got older and started helping out, grandpa would cut me in on the profits. I had a nice little nest egg going for me by the time everything went bad.

BK: I know I'm wasting my time by asking you to jump to the bad part, so why don't you tell me about the things you did to help out.

Tanya: In the beginning, it was mostly just keeping the house clean. After working the fields for a few hours, grandpa would head into the barn and work in there. I'd make him something to eat, usually simple things like sandwiches or canned soup, which I left outside the barn. He would always wait until I was back in the house before he opened the door and took the food inside.

BK: Weren't you curious about what was going on in there?

Tanya: Not really, no. I've never been a nosy person or someone interested in the business of others, so I went about doing what grandpa asked. I did mention schooling to him when I learned that other kids my age were going, but he said that he could teach me the important things in life, none of which they taught in schools, according to him. He always found time to read to me though, as well as making sure that I could read and write. I wasn't ever going to get into no college, but I knew enough to get by. Plus, I figured that with my good looks, I could land myself a wealthy man without too much trouble. I thought that life would be easy once I was grown up and living in the big city with a successful husband who took care of my every need.

BK: Yet, you are still here. Why is that?

Tanya: I needed to look after grandpa, but I'm getting to that. Anyway, when he figured I was old enough, which was when I turned sixteen, as I remember it, he told me that he wanted to show me what was in the barn. I wasn't that impressed by what I saw if I'm being honest. I think I had built it up to be something more, but the interior was nothing more than a bunch of water tanks ringing the interior, as well as a few card tables like they have in the casino, although not quite as fancy. There was also some strange looking equipment at the back of the barn, which he told me was where he made the moonshine.

During the day, he would have me scrub the water tanks and make sure that they were always sparkling clean. At night, men would come from all over to play cards, which, like drinking, was also illegal. I would be on hand to serve grandpa's moonshine to the gamblers, which further increased my savings since the winners were always ready to hand over a tip if I kept the drinks coming. Grandpa also had a side business where he would loan money to the men who were losing or couldn't afford the buy-in. Many of those men ended up signing over their watches, rings, and even their car if things got out of control. Grandpa was fair but tough, and he had a couple of big men from the next town over on the payroll, just in case someone got the idea not to pay back what he was owed.

BK: Didn't the cops know what he was up to?

Tanya: The police were among his best customers. They were extended a bigger line of credit than most, plus they got the occasional bottle of moonshine to take home with them. These were all local men that liked a drink and some fun as much as the next man, so they weren't about to put grandpa out of business.

BK: Did the men behave themselves around you? I mean, did they ever try to do anything inappropriate?

Tanya: That depends what your idea of inappropriate is. I played the game a little, knowing that I would make more money if I was friendly with the gents. I'd gladly suffer a pat on the butt or a little squeeze here and there, but grandpa made damn sure that no-one would ever go further than that. One time, a man made a move to put his hands between my legs, and it turned ugly right quick. Grandpa used to walk around with a cane, which he didn't need, and he would use it wherever he saw fit. The handle was made of brass and cut into the shape of a goose head. It was a hard, heavy piece of metal that could do damage when swung the right way. Grandpa hit that man upside the head with that thing and then set his two goons on him. He came back a couple of weeks later, still all bruised and cut up around the face, and he apologized to me before going back to his cards. The touching slowed right down after that, although a couple of others tried it on, always with the same result.

BK: It sounds as though your grandpa was protective of you.

Tanya: Only when he thought I had been treated badly. He raised me to look after myself, but there were some things that he would not stand back and watch. He was always respectful to the ladies, at least as far as I saw, but he lost his way when he brought that bitch home. Heck, all the men did. She was bad business.

All the men in our town and the neighboring towns loved my grandpa for the services that he provided, but they almost all said that the barn would be a whole lot better if women were on the menu. He would laugh when the subject was raised but would always say that he wasn't no pimp. Imagine my surprise when I go out to clean up the barn, and there's a half-naked lady tied up in the back corner. Grandpa was sitting in front of her in an old wooden rocking chair, going back and forth and staring at her while she cursed him in some strange language.

BK: Do you know what language she was speaking?

Tanya: I asked grandpa about that, and he told me that it was Creole. You could tell that what she was saying was hateful, but it all sounded so lovely coming out of her mouth.

BK: What else did he tell you about her?

Tanya: He was reluctant to go into a lot of detail about how she ended up in our barn, but what I can tell you is that she had been passing through Redfield with some drifter fella, and it was obvious that they were no good. The local cops took the stranger into custody and suggested that she would be a good addition to the family business. She was certainly a looker, although not nearly as pretty as I am. She had that darker skin, which always looks so ugly to me, plus she was covered in weird markings and tattoos, none of which was very appealing. Not that I'm in the market for no lady, you understand. All I'm doing is explaining what she looked like.

Anyway, grandpa got the word out that we wouldn't be open for business for three days while he decided what to do. He told me to stay out of the barn during that time, so I've no idea what he was up to. I did hear cars come and go in the early hours during that time, and once we opened for business again, the girl was all cleaned up and tucked away in a sealed off area at the back of the barn. Grandpa and his friends must have built that addition while I was kept outside, but I was given the grand tour after the fact.

BK: Why would your grandpa do that?

Tanya: Now, look at you, sweetie, drawing out a story when all you wanted was for it to be over.

BK: Call me naturally curious.

Tanya: He gave me the tour because he wanted me to be in charge of the woman. I had to clean her up, feed her, and make sure that she was splayed out like a Thanksgiving turkey waiting for the stuffing when the barn opened for business. He also told me that since I was doing extra work on her, I should leave the biggest water tank alone and that he would have one of the boys clean that one. I didn't feel right about it at first, but money cures all those feelings right quick, and since I wasn't much of a fan of the tank scrubbing, he had himself a deal. Plus, she was a foul-mouthed hussy. She'd spit at me, curse in all sorts of different tongues, and generally make my life miserable. She had a roof over her head, a bed to sleep on, and three squares a day. I never could figure out what the heck she was complaining about?

BK: Are you serious?

Tanya: From what I saw, all the men were sweet to her. She never had a mark on her when I would clean her up, except for those nasty tattoos. I've never understood why anyone would mess up a perfectly nice body by covering it in yucky ink. I'm a simple country girl with no airs or graces, but I tell you, people covered in tattoos are pure trash.

BK: I have a couple.

Tanya: Then maybe I need to rethink my opinion of them, sweetie. I'm just playing with ya. At least you have the decency to keep them covered up. If you need to have them, put them in a place where they aren't always on show. That's what I think.

BK: We seem to be sliding a little off topic, Tanya. Can we steer it back to your story and talk about what happened after this woman arrived?

Tanya: Well, excuse me. I was enjoying the pleasure of your company, what with you being so handsome and nice, but let's get back to what you want. So, things were going good in terms of business. Grandpa was making a lot of money, which meant that I was too, but things were starting to go south with the wild woman. Some of the men were starting to get spooked, saying that she was casting spells and making them nervous. Some even complained that they couldn't get excited in her presence; you know what I mean?

BK: Of course.

Tanya: Some of the men suggested that grandpa expand that side of the business and offer up a few different girls. The cops seemed keen on lending a hand, saying that they could easily find runaways and hitchhikers who would easily fill that need. Grandpa wasn't about to go for that, though. He said they were all just, pardon my language, pussies who couldn't get it up. He thought all the voodoo talk was nothing but superstitious mumbo-jumbo and said he would prove it by having his way with her. He waited until one night when we had a really big crowd in; he told me to go home and take the rest of the night off, that he had some man business to attend to. Before I took off, he asked me to clean that girl up good and proper and get her ready, which I did, but I also made sure that she wasn't tied up quite so tight that night.

BK: Why would you do that?

Tanya: I was hoping she would get loose and get away. From the moment she arrived, the men stopped paying me as much attention as they used to. She looked at me funny when I was loosening up her bindings and telling her to keep pretending that she was a tied until they were done with her for the night. I'd never heard her speak a single word of English in her time there, but the look on her face told me that she understood every word I was saying to her. I didn't like her at all, sweetie, and would gladly see her suffer, but she was eating into my time and my attention. I made sure she knew that too, knew that I wasn't going all soft and gooey.

BK: So, did she finally escape?

Tanya: She did, but not without creating a scene. I hadn't been in my room long when I heard a commotion coming from over by the barn. When I looked out the window, men were hightailing it out of there, and a few were crying, or at least I thought they were, but I later found out that they were bleeding from the eyes. Grandpa came stumbling out last, his throat cut from ear to ear, and there she was, right behind him and floating a little off the ground.

BK: Floating? Surely you were imagining things.

Tanya: Nuh-uh. I could see the shadow below her feet, and the bindings were trailing behind her as she went through the air. She had her arms spread out like Jesus on the cross, and her eyes were rolled back in her head. The barn went up like a tinderbox the moment she crossed the threshold, and she may have done a sight more damage if one of the cops hadn't put her down with a bullet through the head. A bunch of the men picked her up and tossed her into the fire, and when it was done burning, the only thing left standing was the water tank that grandpa told me to leave alone.

We buried grandpa the day after all this went down, with everyone begging me to promise that I wouldn't say a word. I think the men were worried about me gabbing to their wives, although I think those ladies were all well aware that their men were up to no good. No-one spoke about the barn or that girl after the fact, and I kept my promise to keep my mouth shut.

BK: Until tonight.

Tanya: That's right, sweetie. Now don't that make you feel special? Aren't you glad you waited around to talk to me?

Unknown: I'm thrilled, Tanya. You're done now, so why don't you scurry off and join your friends. I'll chat with you later.

Tanya: Yes, sir.

King of the Road by Unknown

BK: I'm not so sure I should be talking to you. After all, you didn't even get up and grace us with a tune.

Unknown: Ha-ha, that's not my job here, although I have always loved singing and playing music. I prefer the complete live performance as opposed to singing over some cheesy backup track.

BK: What would you have sung, had you been forced to?

Unknown: Are you suggesting the others were forced?

BK: It felt that way. Why would they sing songs that bring up such painful memories of the past? Plus, I've noticed you all night, whispering in their ears and seemingly telling them what to do. What's that about?

Unknown: King of the Road.

BK: What?

Unknown: You asked me what song I would sing if I were to do it karaoke style. King of the Road seems the most fitting to the story that I would tell, but maybe you'll come up with a different tune for me once we reach the end of our time together.

BK: So, (garbled), are you suggesting that you have a story to tell?

Unknown: Why, Mr. Keane, you've heard it already, albeit in snatches and snippets. These people here are nothing but my playthings, doing and saying whatever it is that I tell them to. How about this, Mr.

Keane, how about I tell you the full story behind why we are all here, yourself included. Would that be something that would interest you?

BK: Me? What the hell does any of this have to do with me?

Unknown: Are you truly of the belief that you stumbled upon my establishment through blind luck? Has it not started to sink in that you may have been brought here for a reason other than cataloging some nonsense about shitty bars that no-one will ever visit besides the same cluster of losers who go there to drown their sorrows and leave their sad sack lives behind them for a couple of hours at a time? Is that what you believe, Mr. Keane?

BK: I don't know what to believe anymore.

Unknown: Let me ask you this then. How do you feel, physically and mentally?

BK: I'm tired, and my head feels fuzzy and out of sorts. It's as though I'm having an out of body experience but am fully aware that I am outside myself.

Unknown: Good answer, Mr. Keane. Now, do me a favor and look around and tell me what you see. Really look.

BK: A dive bar, but one no different from the many others that I have been in on this trip.

Unknown: Look closer. The devil is in the details.

BK: I don't know what you want me to look for.

Unknown: Just look and start telling me all that you see.

BK: Um, okay. Besides you and I, there are 10 other people here, all of whom have spoken to me. There isn't anyone behind the bar, and all the bottles there appear to be empty. The "OPEN" sign is flickering off and on, as is the "EXIT" sign, which is stuck on the wall with no door in sight. In fact, I don't see any doors or windows here, yet I regularly feel bright lights hitting me in the face. There is a thin layer of dust settling on everything, and the glass in front of me is half-filled with what looks like dirty river water.

Unknown: Very good, Mr. Keane. Now, does this place look like every other dive bar that you have been in on your journey, or does it look and feel just a touch different?

BK: Different.

Unknown: Next question; how long have you been here?

BK: That's tough to answer. I think I left my phone in the car and since this place doesn't seem to have a clock, my guess would be a few hours.

Unknown: What if I told you it was more like three days?

BK: That's not possible. First off, I wouldn't be able to stay awake for three days, and secondly, my recorder wouldn't hold a charge that long. The red light is still on, which means it's still recording, so my guess would be that you, like the rest of them, are trying to mess with me. What I don't know is why you would do such a thing.

Unknown: Messing with you is certainly not my intent, Mr. Keane, at least not in this lifetime. It seems you are going to take a little convincing, though, so allow me to tell you my story if you will. I believe it might just answer all the questions that I am sure you have. You should feel free to jump in whenever you feel like it, in case you need me to make things clearer. I am a natural storyteller, Mr. Keane, but I have been known to omit details, not always on purpose. There's no need to check your recording device. Trust me, it will continue to work until we are through. Are you ready?

BK: I am.

Unknown: When I was a young man, I dreamed that I would someday be a singer of some renown. My love of music came at a very early age, perhaps born out of the fact that my father always had the radio playing, singing along to the big hits of the day. I would sing along with him, stumbling over the words until I had them all down pat. He never laughed at my mistakes, and he never tried to correct me, choosing instead to let me learn from those subtle tongue slips.

As time went by, I would sing even when the radio was off, which was usually when I was out in the fields helping my father with the farm work. This was usually in the summer months when school was out, as he was a stickler for education, loudly declaring to me that there is more money to be made using your brain than your hands, although I saw the value in both. I enjoyed learning new things at school, but I also loved working the fields and breaking a sweat. But, most of all, I loved singing, with writing coming a close second. I was always trying to come up with new songs that were on a par with those on the radio, and I think I came close a couple of times.

BK: Did you ever share those songs with anyone?

Unknown: Not knowingly, but my mother would hear me humming and singing, and when she found my notes while cleaning my room, she asked that I read some of my lyrics to her. Mother was an avid reader, often re-reading the same few books that we had at home. I was embarrassed to do so at the start, but I saw that my words brought her real joy. She told my father about it, and one night after dinner, they asked if would consider performing an impromptu concert for them. It was tough, but I figured that if I wanted to be a professional singer, I needed to get in the habit of singing in front of people, so I did it.

BK: I can't believe I'm asking, but how did it go?

Unknown: I only sang three or four songs, which were the ones that I had fully formed and which I liked. My mother burst into applause after each song, and by the time I was done, she had tears rolling down her cheeks. My father remained stoic, but he did tell me that he thought I had talent, which was a rave review coming from him. A few days after my performance my father said that he had some business to take care of in town and that I should start work without him.

He was gone a couple hours, and when he returned, he called me over to his truck, telling me that he needed some help. When I got there, he told me to get the stuff in back, which turned out to be one thing; it was a guitar case that held a used, but totally beautiful, acoustic guitar. I was stunned, and my mother, who was obviously in on the decision, was crying once again. My father looked me square in the eye, gave a little smile, and said that I had used my brain to write those songs and that maybe I should use my hands to make music to go with them.

BK: While that sounds like a precious Hallmark moment, at this point I don't give a shit about any of it. I want out of here in the worst way, so why don't you just quit dicking around and get to the point, if there is one.

Unknown: Your interest seems to be waning, Mr. Keane. This is hardly surprising since you are now so close to getting your wish and getting out of here. I suppose I can gloss over many of the details of my childhood, but not the important parts, such as my father losing the farm after my mother passed. He hit the bottle hard and left me to do all the work, which was impossible. There was no money to hire help, so I sang and played guitar in the local joints to make a few extra bucks. I came home from one of those gigs to find my dad hanging in the living room, a foreclosure letter from the bank sitting below him on the floor, covered in the piss that came out of him when his neck snapped. There was no inheritance coming my way save for the clothes I wore, my guitar, and the family truck, which we owned outright. After he was put in the ground, I hit the road and drove as far away from my home as possible.

BK: I want to feel sympathy for you, (garbled), but it seems I just don't have it in me. You still haven't gotten to the part about why we are all here. When is that coming?

Unknown: Look at how bright it is in here now, Mr. Keane. My guess is that I had better get to the meat of my story. Otherwise, you are going to be out of here without ever hearing the end.

BK: Wait. What have the bright lights got to do with any of this? Oh, hell no. Am I dead and going towards the light? Is that what's happening? I don't want to be dead. Please, please put me back where I belong. I promise I'll listen to you talk all night if it means I get to go back.

Unknown: Ha-ha. Stop being so damn melodramatic. I can assure you that you are alive and well. The rest of us here perhaps not so much. Drink your crappy water and listen. We are almost done here.

Now, where was I? Right, so I left town and simply drove as far as I could go on the small amount of money that I had. When I ran out of dough, I would take on an odd job wherever I landed, usually working fields or cleaning up in diners. I'd occasionally sing at local bars, although it was usually for a couple of beers and a roof over my head for the night as opposed to money. Beggars can't be choosers, so I took what I got and was happy, for the most part. In time, I worked my way south and ended up settling in Louisiana for a spell, which was where I met the love of my life, Sabine. This was the 1950's, so a white man consorting with a black woman was still frowned upon, but we didn't care. It helped that she was viewed as a witch, what with her wild shock of hair and her tribal tattoos.

BK: You said the 1950's. How is that even possible?

Unknown: Because that's when it happened. Dates and times are not what's important here, Mr. Keane. As much as I loved Sabine, she was indeed wild and was mixed up in the world of voodoo and witchcraft. She would cleanse houses or create potions and curses for the paying public, but I believed it all to be for show. Her antics started to wear thin, though, and it was soon made clear that we should move on, so we hopped in my truck and went in search of pastures new. Money was tight again, forcing us to make frequent stops so that I could get back to odd jobs.

We should have headed north, but south was where it always seemed warm, and since we often had to sleep under the stars, it was the much better option. I would play my guitar and sing to her every night, often creating new songs that only she would ever hear. Again, life was good, but it all came crashing down around us when we crossed the state line into Georgia and landed in the town of Redfield.

BK: I haven't been able to get a clear picture of what it was like based on what the others have said. Can you tell me more about it?

Unknown: Don't worry about that lot, I'll get to them soon enough. Redfield was nothing more than a bunch of strawberry fields surrounded by houses, eleven of them to be exact. The folks that lived there worked the field and shared the profits, or so they told me. They all looked well off for folks that only worked a few months out the year, so I'm guessing there was something else going on. They took me on when I asked for work, and one of them even let me park out back of their property so that me and Sabine could use the truck as our home.

Things went pretty well, but Sabine kept telling me that we could do better if I would just let her help. I told her that she didn't need to work, but she was talking about something else entirely, saying that she could conjure up spirits that would help me become a famous singer. She'd talk about all the money I would make and how we could live the high life in a proper home of our own. I didn't believe in all that stuff, but I wanted to keep her happy, so I played along and told her to make it happen. That was not a good idea.

BK: What did she do, (garbled)?

Unknown: I knew she was a little off in some ways. We had done some bad shit on our travels to that point, mugging and stealing and basically fucking people over for money, but it was all so that we could survive. Sabine would light up when we did those things, though, and you could tell that she wanted to go a step further. I was always able to talk her down, but the fire in her eyes burned brightly for hours after our misdeeds. She'd get as horny as all hell, too, and would bite and scratch and fuck like a crazy woman. It got to the point where I would look forward to us turning someone over just so I could reap the rewards after the fact.

My giving her permission to do her voodoo thing was more than enough for her. I went back to the truck after work and found her gone. I was concerned something had happened to her, but I soon found a note in the cabin of the truck telling me to head towards a big abandoned barn sitting just beyond the strawberry fields. When I got there, she was naked and dancing around a fire, holding an old tin cup over her head and chanting some Creole tune. That was alarming enough, but it was the sight of the girl all carved open on the ground that snapped me out of my reverie.

BK: Who was the girl?

Unknown: It was the teenage daughter of one of the Redfield families. She was all torn up, as though Sabine had carved her open, which judging by the blood on her hands and face may actually have been what went down. I asked her what she was doing, and she said she was casting the spell that would bring fame and fortune my way. I knew that if we didn't get out of there right at that moment, death would be the only thing coming our way. She said she wasn't leaving until the spell was cast, which meant I had to drink the blood from the tin cup. It was madness, plain and simple, but she always could make me do anything she asked. Perhaps it was the hypnotic look in her eyes, or maybe it was the sight of her sweat coating that beautiful body, but whatever it was, I drank, and I drank it all. She knelt down and kissed the dead girl on the forehead, thanking her for her offerings, and then we headed back towards the truck.

The families were all outside by that point, calling for the girl, and I knew then that we were fucked. They saw us coming, and there was nowhere to run or hide. There was also no excuse, as we were both painted in blood. The men, as well as a few of the women, were on us in a flash, beating the shit out of us and demanding to know what we had done. Sabine laughed through it all, but I caved in and pointed in the direction of the barn.

BK: I don't understand any of this. It can't be real. Wake up, wake up, wake up...

Unknown: They got us back to the barn and tied us up good and tight. They took the dead girl away and left us alone for a while, but they were all business when they came back. We were informed that a family vote had been taken and that by a count of 10-1, we were to be punished for our sins. They took their time about it, and they were incredibly thorough.

BK: Not listening anymore. That's enough.

Unknown: They started out slow, each of the adult men taking a turn with Sabine while two of the women held my head and forced me to watch. They knew that since I had been in the fields all day, that she was the ringleader, which is why she probably got the worst of it. Once they were done defiling her, they used hammers to crush her hands, slapping her awake whenever she threatened to pass out. Her legs were next to get the hammer treatment, the bones breaking the skin and popping out with each new blow. I screamed then, which was when they started carving off pieces of her flesh and forcing them down my throat.

BK: No. These are their stories. These are the things they told me.

Unknown: The story is all mine, Mr. Keane, and I've been telling it to them for a long time now. When it was obvious that Sabine was almost gone, they took my knife and stabbed her through the neck, after which they untied her and dumped her in an old water tank at the back of the barn. The last thing I remember from that world is seeing the scythe come rushing towards me. I'm told that my truck was stripped of the paint and all other markings and placed in the middle of the strawberry fields, my head propped on the scarecrow as a warning to anyone else thinking of fucking with the families. My body was dumped in the tank of an old crop duster that had long since stopped flying, and that was the end of all that.

BK: How can you possibly know what happened if you were killed? What do you mean someone told you after the fact?

KARAOKE NIGHT

Unknown: Are you a religious man, Mr. Keane?

BK: No, not at all.

Unknown: You may want to rethink that and get right with God. Or, you could continue your heathen ways and take a trip downstairs to spend eternity with my main man.

BK: No. What? No.

Unknown: There was only one place I was going after how I had lived my life, so it's probably no real surprise to learn that I took the downward path. It seems, though, that my beloved Sabine was not crazy after all. Her spell worked in a way, and rather than spending an eternity in some serious hurt, I was granted a reprieve of sorts. The Devil liked the cut of my jib and made me an offer that was impossible to refuse. Rather than being pulled into Hell's hard labor, I was sent here and given the opportunity to fuck with some folks in any way that I saw fit.

BK: Is this purgatory?

Unknown: No. This is my own private playground, where the only people invited are the family members of the people who did me and Sabine wrong. They all pass through here. Some stay a while before being sent to the big man, while others I keep around. There are even a couple of the original family members in here.

BK: How do you decide who stays and who goes, and why this? Why the whole karaoke thing?

Unknown: One of my punishments is that I don't get to play music anymore. It may seem small to you, but Sabine, my music, and that old guitar were what

I loved most. I may not have that, but I can still create my own little greatest hits albums down here by making them sing the songs I like. The music never ends here, and while I am allowed to shut them out and listen to all the songs in the world, which is one of my rewards for being so very naughty, they are forced to sing the songs I tell them to, over and over again. I create stories for them to think about while they sing, usually some awful tale involving one of the family members that has already passed through. You know how annoying it is when you get a song stuck in your head, right? Imagine never having it leave and imagine that it's associated with an awful life event. It's not torture on the scale of what my Master has to offer, but it makes me happy seeing them suffer.

BK: How do I fit into all of this, and why have them essentially tell your story to me?

Unknown: Let's begin with the reason why I keep some and send others on their way, shall we, Mr. Keane? I have always loved those albums where there is an underlying theme or where a story is told in linear fashion through the songs on there. When I had the chance to bring you here, I decided to create an album with a theme — one that also told my story. You see, Brian, the only family that voted to keep Sabine and myself alive so that we could be taken to the police was the Keane family, your not so distant relatives.

BK: NO!

Unknown: Yes, Mr. Keane. They moved away from Redfield that very night and never returned. They also banished that part of their history from their lives, refusing ever to pass the story on down. Your grandparents were young then, and since they are both still alive, I have never had a chance to thank them for their part in my story properly. You are a storyteller, much like I am, Mr. Keane, so I felt you deserved the opportunity to hear your family history in a creative way. Since you cannot stay, I assume that the good deed performed by your grandparents means that none of the Keane's will be spending any more time here.

BK: The theme. What about the theme for this album?

Unknown: Look at how bright it has suddenly become, Mr. Keane. It looks like it's time for you to go. As for the theme, simply look to the names. That is why I kept this group around for you.

Outro

It is now where I should come clean about parts of my story that I left out in the intro. I did not do so with the intent to deceive, but rather to make it easier for you to attack the content with an open mind.

While I really do remember nothing of my lost days, I do have some details to pass on after the fact. My wife contacted the authorities after 24 hours with no contact from me, and they started looking for me from the point where the GPS on my phone showed me to be before the battery died. My vehicle was found in a ditch about thirty miles from the GPS location. The way it had gone off the road made it tough for passing vehicles, what little there were, to see it even though their headlights must surely have crossed its path.

When the car was found, I wasn't inside. They followed some blood drops and found me in a field, my head bust open, apparently from hitting my head on the steering wheel, and my digital recorder in my hand. They were more than a little surprised to find me alive but surmised that I had made it by drinking muddy rainwater and eating strawberries from a plant that was growing wild there.

They got me out of there, and after a couple of days in the hospital, I was sent home. It wasn't until a few weeks after being back that my wife brought up the recorder and asked why I had dragged it with me into the field. I had no idea and no recollection of having it on me when I was found, so I was as bemused as she was. We decided to listen together and became more and more distressed with each passing interview. It was my wife's idea to write it all down and shop it to publishers, which I did, expecting zero response. Imagine my surprise when multiple offers came in. My disappearance made the national news for a minute, so the publishers figured I would be an easy sell to the buying public.

I expected to go through a laborious editing process, but they liked the idea of keeping the transcripts intact, albeit with a few minor changes. While I had the audio to prove that I had indeed been talking to people during those three days, I decided to embrace the belief of the publisher and look at it from a fiction standpoint. I changed some of the details and switched the order of the stories around, creating a timeline and history of Redfield that made more sense, to me at least. They dismissed those changes immediately, suggesting, or should I say demanding, that I leave things well enough alone.

I had been presented with a very nice advance for the rights to the book and was not about to give that up, especially if it meant not having to spend countless hours editing and rewriting. As I was about to send in the final draft, my wife brought up the final moment in the interview with the unknown man, specifically about what he meant by the names. We went over all the song titles, believing that was what he was talking about. We looked at the release dates looking for clues and even tried to use weird ciphers to decode some sort of hidden meaning in the titles.

We were about to give up when we once again questioned why the order of the stories seemed to be important. It was then that the theme became apparent in the names of the people telling the tales: Paul, Ursula, Neil, Ian, Susan, Harold, Marie, Eric, Norm, and Tanya. Look at the first initial in those names and the theme appears: P-U-N-I-S-H-M-E-N-T. It was all so simple and staring us in the face the whole time, but you fail to see it when you want to believe that something isn't real.

Acknowledgments

As always, I need to thank my wife Penny for her patience during the writing process. I'm not the most pleasant person to be around when the creative juices are flowing. A big thank you to all my friends and family who read the initial draft and offered creative criticism and honest feedback. A big shout out to Matt Frankel, my drinking buddy and good friend, for taking the time to create a cover for me. Finally, a huge thank you to Jeffrey Miller for agreeing to write the foreword.

About the Author

Robots, clowns, and living statues are among the extensive list of things that terrify author John Watson. He is of the belief that writing about these horrors will make him immune to their evils, but the cure is still a work in progress. Watson spends most of his time hiding out in the closet space beneath the stairs, where he is currently working on a series of scary short stories. He has published *Karaoke Night* and a short story in Crazy Ink Publishing's anthology *Infamy,* but has others in the works for 2019 and 2020 with Crazy Ink Publishing.

He resides in Atlanta with his chef wife Penny and a pair of equally skittish fur babies.

Horror Author John Watson

Follow John Watson at:

Web: www.authorjohnwatson.com

Facebook: facebook.com/authorjohnwatson

Instagram: Instagram.com/authorjohnw

Twitter: twitter.com/authorjohnw

CRAZY
INK

Copyright © 2019 by Crazy Ink
Edits by Samantha Talarico

All rights reserved. No part of this publication may be reproduced, distributed or transmitted in any form or by any means, without prior written permission.

Publisher's Note: This is a work of fiction. Names, characters, places, and incidents are a product of the author's imagination. Locales and public names are sometimes used for atmospheric purposes. Any resemblance to actual people, living or dead, or to businesses, companies, events, institutions, or locales is completely coincidental.

Book Layout by Crazy Ink